Peggy,
It's that time of the year again. I find X-mas always ... dont remember if I've given you or if you've already read them. this one looks good! Merry X-mas.
Love,
Sandy

P.S.
Happy reading!
ox
X-mas 2000

# LITTLE
# ELLIE
# CLAUS

# LITTLE ELLIE CLAUS

## James Manos, Jr.

POCKET BOOKS
New York London Toronto Sydney Singapore

POCKET BOOKS, a division of Simon & Schuster, Inc.
1230 Avenue of the Americas, New York, NY 10020

Copyright © 2000 by James Manos, Jr.

ISBN: 0-7434-0624-9

First Pocket Books hardcover printing November 2000

10   9   8   7   6   5   4   3   2   1

POCKET and colophon are registered trademarks of Simon & Schuster, Inc.

Interior illustrations by Hilda Stark Manos

Printed in the U.S.A.

*This book is dedicated to my wife,*
*Hilda*
*who is as beautiful and unique*
*as a fragile snowflake.*
*Thank you my love.*
*And to my sweet, gentle children,*
*Lucy, Charlotte, Peter, and Ellie*
*who know*
*and still believe in the goodness of the heart.*

## ACKNOWLEDGMENTS

To Donna Carolan, whose dedicated support gave me the necessary building blocks to bring life to this book. My wholehearted gratitude and appreciation goes to her.

Paul Fedorko, my book agent, whose enthusiasm and insight not only propelled me forward, but opened the door into this new world. If it weren't for him, I never would have been in the house of—

Judith Curr, publisher of Pocket Books, who I thank for letting me in. Which brings me to the man who gave me my foundation:

My attorney and friend, Bill Jacobson: the first person I met in Hollywood and the last man I'll see when it's time to lock up the doors and go back home. Thank you.

Bruce Brown, my film agent, whose carpeted floors I love to roll around on—

Paul Schnee, a wonderful and careful editor, who sweetened the brief cup of tea we shared, and to Tracy Sherrod, whose patience and invaluable help will long be remembered.

But never to be forgotten is—

The home I came from. My family in New York. Joanne and John, Ellen and Peter, and especially, my mother, Jo. I am indeed blessed.

And finally to my father—who, as I write this, is without question inventing or tinkering with some new toy with my little sister Christina somewhere up in the North Pole.

God bless them all.

# Part One

## Christmas, 1933

## ONE

What a racket! People walking on the sidewalks turned and grimaced, then smacked their hands against their ears in agony as the old, weather-beaten jalopy of a pickup truck sputtered and coughed its way down the congested streets of Manhattan's Lower East Side. The back of the truck was packed as high as the eye could see with wooden boxes and a bunch of secondhand furniture lashed together with twine. Swinging off the sides of the whole rickety kit and caboodle were countless birdcages filled with frenzied, chirping birds eager to get off that billowing heap of smoke and hightail it out of New York and back to the small town of Winterset, Iowa, where their journey had begun. And without a doubt, the good-looking newlyweds, stuffed inside their truck on that cool autumn day, were thinking the same thing.

Never in their lives had they seen so many people,

buildings, images, and things crammed together. Born and raised on a couple of farms, Peter and Lucy's notion of "crowded" meant jamming an extra chair against their kitchen table when a couple of their neighbors unexpectedly showed up for some supper. Peter and Lucy were always happy to oblige. The pot was passed, smiles all around, and life went on. But how did life exist here, wondered the pretty but delicate twenty-year-old Lucy as she sat in the passenger seat, stuffed between suitcases and animal cages filled with little hamsters, guinea pigs, turtles, a few small aquariums with all sorts of hysterical fish flapping about, even a baby marsupial or two—making one thing clear to anyone who might have looked inside, that these two liked their pets.

Lucy twisted uncomfortably in her passenger seat, picked the pussycat (whom they regally named Montclair-Sinclair-Éclair) off her lap, and gently reached over and stroked her husband's hair as he drove with tense determination. He too was striking, with finely chiseled features, a thick shock of dark hair combed back, and like his wife, had soft, gentle-looking eyes. Certainly Peter and Lucy had an unusual bond and much in common. They had met way back in the third grade and decided right there and then they were going to marry, exchanged their vows during recess, and when they each ran home that day and told their parents, their folks just shook their heads and said, "Well, we'll see." But the parents knew. They could see it in their children's eyes: portholes to decency and politeness, forgiveness and trust. Lucy and Peter saw the world not with judgment but with wonder, and when they looked at each other, their eyes registered more than love—they radiated a heartwarming adoration for each other. They were lucky.

Peter gave her a quick reaffirming look, as if to say, Don't worry, sweetie, we'll find where we're going sooner or later. But privately, he thought to himself, My God, we're never going to make it, this place looks like it's been hit by a twister. He directed his attention back to the congested streets and saw people everywhere hawking and selling anything and everything: rags, pieces of tin, clothes and hats, pots and pans, pencils and food. Vendors with pushcarts warmed their mittie-gloved hands on the steam rising from the piping-hot corn-on-the-cob and cooked sweet potatoes they were selling for a nickel. "Just a nickel . . . please!" they screamed. Merchants and fishmongers waved unidentifiable fish over their heads. . . . Fish? More like sea monsters, Lucy and Peter thought. Back where they came from, meat was the staple. Fat Harry down the road always had the best corn-fed cattle, and Buck-Toothed Jake was famous for his blue-ribboned hogs, and of course, everyone else had their own chickens for the pickings. Sure, they hooked an occasional bass or two out of the lake. But what the heck were they selling here in New York? That fish back there had whiskers as long as golden straw framing its gaping mouth. Dismayed, they immediately diverted their attention to the vegetable and fruit men pushing wagons piled as high as haystacks with wilted cauliflower and bruised, rotten apples, and they almost gagged.

Sweating now, Peter slowly navigated his rig along-side horse-drawn carriages and more powerful trucks with tough, brawny-looking delivery men, honking and screaming for the little kids scampering across the street to quickly get out of their way. But Lucy saw something curious. She noticed the outright defiance of the little ruffians as they scooted like jackrabbits in and out of the street grabbing little chunks of black "gold" that must have bounced off the coal truck earlier that morning. Crossing a Roman chariot race would have been easier, she thought. But these kids, the nimble and fearless, knew that capturing a few pieces of coal, which now lay glistening in the midst of certain oncoming death, meant more than a couple of fried eggs on the stove or a moment's worth of hand-smacking warmth back in their cold, damp, overcrowded tenements. The coal was a life source—it gave them hope and it was the least they could do to contribute to their household without get-ting pinched by the coppers for stealing an apple or a loaf of bread. In desperate times like these, nothing was wasted, and that thought was not wasted on Lucy.

It was clear to her that in this year of 1933, life in the city had been reduced to its lowest denominator—make a dollar any way you can to eat, pay the rent, feed the family, put some clothes on their backs, as everyone was struggling and suffering under the weight of the Great Depression. As Lucy and Peter continued to wonder how everyone managed, a look of concern crossed both their faces when they saw an old man, a beggar sitting cross-legged on the sidewalk, selling a bent and rusted fork. How sad, they thought, until they saw another more unfortunate-looking old lady bend over and buy that fork from the beggar.

"They'd never believe it," she said softly.

Afraid to take his wide-opened peepers off the road for too long, Peter shot her a quick look and mumbled, "Who's that?"

"My folks. I wish they were alive to see it."

"Mine too," said Peter sadly.

But they couldn't. Their parents had died a long time ago, leaving them alone as they entered into this new world of New York City. But in order to start their new life, they first needed to find where they were going, which was 314 East 8th Street, and it wasn't looking easy. In fact, it was starting to look downright impossible.

Peter adjusted his wool cap, wiped his brow. "I just hope we find our apartment before this ol' truck gives out."

Lucy moved Montclair-Sinclair-Éclair off her lap, reached down by her feet, and retrieved a crumpled map.

"I think it's right around the corner."

"Let's hope so," said Peter, breathing hard.

He turned the heavy steering wheel, hand over hand, rounded the corner, and sputtered down a tenement-lined street. They peered through the windshield and stared in amazement at all the tenements looming ominously over them.

"Where's the sky?" asked Lucy.

"I guess they don't need it here," whispered Peter.

As the truck rumbled over the cobblestones, spewing smoke all over the place, Peter and Lucy eyed the rusty fire escapes rising up into the sky, all packed with people. Some were scrubbing their clothes, others sleeping on dirty mattresses, while others just leaned over the railing gasping for a breath of fresh air. In Iowa, Lucy thought, everything is firmly on the ground and one always knew where one stood. When we looked into the sky it was just to see the storm clouds brewing, the morning sun, the starry nights. Never did we look up expecting to see people.

Lucy turned to Peter, her voice now laced with concern. "My God, do you think we made the right decision?"

Peter glanced at her and wanted to scream out: NO! THIS IS CRAZY! WE SHOULD RUN, RUN AWAY! But he didn't. Instead, he kept mum while his eyes caught the sight of a rundown tenement.

"I think we found it," he said thankfully, pulling the jalopy over to the curb, where it spat, coughed, gurgled, and then with a sudden rush of smoke coming out of its exhaust pipe came to a complete stop. Relieved, they leaned in for a kiss and then—BAM. Startled, they looked up and saw an old, veiny fist attached to the sinewy arm of a skeletal-looking old shrew, punching the hood of the car.

"GET THAT JALOPY OUTTA MY SPOT OR I'LL CALL THE COPPERS!"

And both Lucy and Peter shuddered as they looked into the old woman's bloodshot green eyes bulging out of her skull.

Montclair-Sinclair-Éclair hissed, swelled to the size of a porcupine, and jumped back onto Lucy's lap, as Lucy trembled in fright. She quickly slammed the door locks down and screamed: "Peter, do something, I've heard about people like this!"

"It's okay, honey. I'll talk to her," he said confidently. He pushed on the door and it creaked open.

He stepped out of the truck and stole a quick glance at the shrew, who remained on the sidewalk, coiled and ready to spring. She eyed his sweat-stained blue work shirt and his worn and tattered dungarees and she wasn't impressed. Peter came closer, and just as he was about to open his mouth, she snorted in disgust, then hissed: "HEY, PAL! YOU DEAF? I SAID IT'S RE-SERVED!"

Peter was shocked. Never in his life had he ever seen anyone quite like this; certainly he never heard a woman bleat like an angry farm animal before. But this is New York, he thought, maybe everyone spoke like this.

"Now hold on a second . . . ," he said.

"That's it!" she shrieked, before jamming her skinny fingers into her mouth to whistle loud for the copper lazily spinning his baton as he walked down the street.

"OFFICER!"

Lucy rolled her window down, yelled out, "Peter, be careful! This might be some kind of scam."

"Scam . . . ?" Peter mouthed in disbelief. Then he thought, If it were a *real* scam, we wouldn't know it, so it couldn't be. Nope, this woman in front of me is just crazy.

"Yes, a scam," Lucy persisted, "I heard about this type of thing on the radio . . ."

"Honey, please—" he began, but he saw the fear in her eyes, so he turned back around, whipped off his hat, and gripped it tight in his hand.

"You still here?" the old witch cried.

Peter looked at her, took a breath, then finally and politely said, "Look, this is 314 East 8th Street, right?"

"Yeah, so what of it?" she spat out.

Peter saw some spittle hanging around her chin, and his first instinct was to point and say, Excuse me, ma'am, but you have a little spittle going on over there by your lip . . . yes, right there . . . But he didn't.

"Well, this is where I'm supposed to be," he said instead.

The skinny shrew coughed and Peter quickly covered his face with his hat, but it was too late. He felt something moist dripping down his cheek and he thought, my God, I just contracted a half dozen medically unknown diseases and he wanted to dive into a vat of alcohol, but he couldn't, so he carefully and slowly wiped his face with his hat.

"You're Peter Thompson?" she said suspiciously.

"Yes, ma'am, and that's my wife, Lucy, right there in the truck. The one you've scared the be Jesus out of."

The skeletal nag slowly leaned like a serpent to her side, eyed Lucy like she was easy prey, sucked on her teeth, then trained her skeptical eyes back on Peter.

"You're that animal doctor from Iowa?"

Feeling pretty good now, Peter smiled wide. "Yes, . . . I mean, no. I'm that guy but I'm not a doctor yet."

"No kidding," she said abruptly, scrutinizing his less than professional clothes.

"I'm a teacher's assistant, getting my degree. I start school in just a couple of days."

"Well, where've you been?" she said, softening. "You know how many people I had to threaten to keep this damn spot open?"

"Well, we're here now," he said excitedly.

"Then this is my lucky day, isn't it?" she said sarcastically.

Peter whipped around, faced his frightened wife. "Sweetheart, come on out, come on over. It's okay, really, it's okay!"

And as Lucy kicked and shoved at the passenger door, Peter turned back to the old hag.

"Then you must be Miss Hardwick. You received our confirmation wire?"

"*Mrs.* Hardwick to you, even though my lousy, good-for-nothing husband is dead and, no . . . I didn't get your fancy schmanzy confirmation wire, so you better call those thieves at Western Union and get your money back. Now, are we all square?"

"Sure, I guess," he said agreeing, but not really sure what he was agreeing to.

Lucy walked over, grabbed her husband's hand.

"Honey, this is Mrs. Hardwick, our new landlady."

"It's a pleasure to meet you." She took Mrs. Hardwick's hand and froze. It felt like a bird's talons, hard and cold, and Lucy quickly pulled her hand away.

Mrs. Hardwick smiled, then gave her a once-over with her big ol' green eyes, saying slyly, "Well aren't you just a fragile little thing."

Lucy wasn't sure how to respond, so she kept quiet and smiled weakly.

"You pay the first of every month," Hardwick said sharply to Peter.

"That's no problem."

"Better not be. This ain't a charity house. Fifth floor. End of the hall. Door's open."

"Sounds great," Lucy said, trying her best to remain as pleasant as she was brought up to be.

"It's a regular Taj Mahal. . . . Now, you better hurry and get all your belongings inside. These are desperate times. Don't want to leave your stuff out for too long."

"Right away," said Peter, and he and Lucy ran back to the truck, not so much to start unpacking but to get as far away from their landlady as quickly as they could. Peter began untying the birdcages and Lucy grabbed the cat when Hardwick shot her arms up like a conductor and screamed, "HOLD IT!"

Peter and Lucy froze; in fact, the whole block seemed to stop moving. They turned slowly around.

"I noticed them before. What the heck are they?" Hardwick said, pointing to the birdcages and all the other animals.

"Parrots," Peter said matter-of-factly.

"A pussycat?" said Lucy, holding Montclair-Sinclair-Éclair.

"You selling 'em?" Hardwick asked suspiciously.

"They're our pets," said Peter, shocked at the question.

"A buck a week extra."

"But . . . ," protested Lucy.

"But nothing. Take it or leave it," she said firmly. Then she cracked a wicked smile and put out her hand.

"And in advance . . . Mr. fancy farm boy."

Peter and Lucy exchanged looks and silently mouthed to each other, "Mr. fancy farm boy?"

Peter quickly rummaged through his pocket, pulled out a few bucks, walked slowly back to her, and gingerly placed the cash in her opened palm. Her fingers snapped over it and the cash disappeared into her housecoat so fast that Peter and Lucy could have sworn they heard the "ka-ching" of a cash register drawer slamming shut.

"Welcome to New York," Hardwick said, and she flipped the key to Peter, who caught it in midair. And before they could say anything else, Hardwick spun around, climbed the stoop stairs, then with her arms straight out, slammed through the front door of her tenement.

Shaking their heads, Peter and Lucy began to unpack their truck again, when out from behind some parked cars a scruffy little homeless mutt of a dog with large pleading eyes trotted up to Peter. He leaned down and let the affection-starved dog lick his face like an ice cream cone.

"Don't even think about it," Lucy said admonishingly.

And Peter just looked at his beautiful wife and laughed with glee.

# TWO

The scraggly mutt now stood proudly in the center of their little apartment. And Mrs. Hardwick was right—it wasn't much and it was definitely small. There was a little icebox in the corner, a stand-up cast-iron bathtub in the middle of the kitchen, a small potbelly stove, and a couple of windows overlooking the courtyard, and that was it. But in just a week's time, they had filled it with books, canned goods stocked high on the kitchen shelves, a comfy little bed tucked in the corner, a small dresser next to it, and a couple of mismatched chairs against a little table covered with an oilcloth in the middle of the room. For Peter and Lucy, along with their parrots, the cat, Montclair-Sinclair-Éclair, a couple of turtles in small aquariums, a few fish bowls, and their new friend, the mangy dog, which they named Rodger-Dodger-the-Podger, it was home sweet home, and all in all, it was pretty darn cozy.

"You're going to be late, honey," Lucy nervously said as she plunked down a bowl of oatmeal on the table.

The bathroom door popped open and Peter, looking very sharp in his suit and tie, patted himself down. "So, how do I look?"

Impressed, Lucy smiled. "Like the real McCoy."

"Like a million bucks?" he said, egging her on.

"More like the new teacher's assistant who's going to get fired because he's late on the first day. Now sit. You don't want to start the day on an empty stomach."

Peter walked to the table, sat down, and started gobbling up the oatmeal in his bowl. With his mouth full, he looked up. "Sure miss those farm eggs."

But Lucy didn't respond; she was too preoccupied, scampering about the apartment, making sure everything was just right for Peter's first day at his new job.

"I made you a little sandwich for lunch," she said, dropping a small wax-papered sandwich next to him on the table. "And don't forget to keep your head up, stand straight, say yes sir, no sir . . ." Then she threw up her hands in mock exasperation and said, "Oh, what am I saying, you're going to charm everyone."

Peter smiled, kicked his chair back, stood, then proudly proclaimed, "I'm off to the races."

All the birds, dogs, cats, hamsters, and whatever else was capable of making a noise started cheering in their own language. Lucy hushed them, then quickly walked around Peter and fixed his jacket collar.

"What time will you be home?" she asked.

"I'm not," he said as he marched toward the door, where he grabbed his coat and fedora off the hook, ceremoniously slapped his hat on his head, and smiled at her.

Lucy paused, wiped the hair back off her face. "Why? What are you scheming?"

Peter grinned, walked slowly, confidently, back to her. "We're stepping out tonight, sweetheart. We're celebrating our new life." He did a little tap dance, then he took her into his arms.

"Drinks at the Stork Club!" she said beaming.

"Dinner at 21!" he said, topping her.

"Take in all the sights!"

"You betcha, my love!" He was barely able to contain himself.

She kissed his cheeks. "And the Empire State Building!"

He kissed her back. "The Waldorf Astoria!"

"The Statue of Liberty!"

"Coney Island!"

"Whattaya say . . . ?"

"Whattaya know!"

Peter lifted her off her feet and twirled her around their little apartment. "Whatever and wherever you want, my love. Yessiree Bob! It's going to be a regular twister." And he gently put her down.

They kissed. Lucy looked into his eyes and with her voice filled with hope said, "Oh, Peter, do you think . . . ?"

"Of course, doll," he replied confidently. "There's no stopping us now." He kissed her hand like she was a princess, she curtsied, and they laughed. He reached for the sandwich on the table, jammed it into his pocket, and ran toward the door.

"Wait! Wait! Where are we meeting?"

He spun around. "The Plaza Hotel."

"Peter!" she said, shocked.

"We're going on a buggy ride."

"And dinner?" she asked coyly.

"Maybe some hot dogs."

"No champagne?" she said in mock disappointment.

"We'll split a bottle of Coke."

Lucy looked him over.

"Come here, Mr. Big Spender."

And he slid back into her arms, where they stood entwined together, staring into each other's eyes. Lucy leaned in closer, their lips almost touching, and whispered, "When was the last time I told you how much I love you?"

"This morning, but tell me again."

Lucy took a breath, and her words fluttered in his ears like soft rose petals. "I love you . . . more than all the cornfields in Iowa."

Peter smiled, hugged her tighter. "And I love you more than all the snowflakes that have ever fallen."

"I like that one better," she said softly. She melted into his arms, and as they kissed, the world came to a gentle stop and the sun bathed them with warmth, and with their eyes closed tight, they both wished the moment would never end. But it did, because all their crazy pets started bleating, squawking, and chirping like mad again. With their cheeks still aglow, Lucy and Peter hushed them quiet.

"See you at seven," he said, gently stroking her hair. He turned away, leaned down and patted the panting Rodger-Dodger-the-Podger on his head, and walked out the door. Lucy smiled, then spun around and started getting ready for the day.

✳

# THREE

Bursting with excitement, Peter tipped his hat with aplomb to everyone he passed as he charged up Broadway. He wanted to run or even skip, but he knew he shouldn't. One mustn't appear too eager, he thought. So he took a deep breath, slowed his legs down, and concentrated on each and every step, but before he knew it, he was running again. You'd better calm down, he chided himself as he slowed to an almost normal gait. And don't forget to stand up straight, say yes sir, no sir . . . recalling Lucy's gentle hints for success, and he laughed aloud remembering how she threw up her hands and exclaimed, *"Oh, what am I saying, you're going to charm everyone."* And with that delightful endorsement from his incredible wife, his heart leapt and he took off running again, cruising right past the guard posting sentry at the formidable gate of Columbia University, past undergrads and grads, their arms filled with boxes and books, and he didn't stop running until he was out of breath and deep in the heart of the campus.

Calmer now, he entered the building of Veterinarian Medicine and walked down the polished wood floors, taking the time to admire the portraits of famed deans, researchers, and veterinarians whom he had idolized growing up. He paused in humble deference, realizing for the first time that he was now (with lots of hard work and a little luck) about to embark on a journey that one day might lead to his own portrait hanging on these very walls, and his heart swelled with the thought. Then he stepped in front of the great Sir Edward Carolan, took off his hat and paid a silent homage to the man who first discovered the cure for Cockatoo gout. And next to him was Dr. William Brown, who as a seventy-year-old man and nearly blind himself, perfected glasses for cataract-afflicted horses. And there, Peter gasped, was the cast-iron bust of Dr. Robert Jacobson, who not only diagnosed and identified the warthog's dismal lack of self-esteem, but through painstaking work, helped those poor misunderstood beasts achieve their full potential, freeing them to live, love, and play, to this very day, with guilt-free confidence on the African plains. What a man, he thought. What a great humanitarian. That's right, Peter said to himself with pride. A humanitarian! What's good for the animal kingdom is good for all humanity, or to put it another way, what's good for the goose is . . . but he didn't finish the thought because he realized he was running late, so he dashed down the long corridor, and within a flash, came upon the frosted glass door that read: "DR. STEPHENSON— DEAN OF VETERINARIAN SCHOOL OF MEDI- CINE." He quickly checked the knot on his tie, tapped gently on the glass, then let himself in.

People were everywhere. Secretaries and assistants, men in white lab coats and suits, workers in blue uni- forms, were all busily packing boxes, emptying filing cab- inets, taking the pictures off the walls. Peter approached a young woman standing by the door with a clipboard in her hand, checking off items with mechanical effi- ciency. Her dark gray suit fitted her with such precision that Peter thought she looked all sealed in—her hair was perfectly combed back, and her nose and mouth were pointed and pinched.

He leaned in. "Checking the list to see who is naughty or nice?"

The woman turned around, glowered at Peter, and said with disdain, "Excuse me?"

Taken aback, Peter quickly smiled. "Just joking. I'm here to see Dean Stephenson."

The woman examined Peter from head to toe, then said haughtily, "You mean, *Dr.* Stephenson." But what she really wanted to say was, Who the heck is this freshly shaved hayseed, wearing a cheap suit, with a wax papered onion and sardine sandwich probably stuffed in his pocket interrupting *me* while I perform this very special and important task of checking items off my neatly organized and printed list? My God, they will let *anyone* into New York these days. But she didn't. Instead she continued with, "The Doctor is back there." And with a quick, impatient point toward the back of the room, she simultaneously directed and dismissed Peter from her life.

Peter mumbled, "Thanks," scooted by her, and she quickly resumed checking her list.

Peter walked through the room, artfully avoiding getting crushed by crates and lamps, heavy boxes, and pieces of furniture lifted high in the air by the workers, until he finally saw a couple of brawny men slide a large mahogany desk off to the side, revealing an elderly pipe-smoking gentleman in a double-breasted wool suit, sitting cross-legged and alone in his chair.

"Excuse me, Dr. Stephenson?"

The Dean looked up.

"I'm Peter Thompson and it's a genuine honor to meet you, sir," Peter said excitedly but with deference.

Momentarily surprised, the Dean stood and extended his hand.

"Thank you. Awful decent of you to come by," he said evenly. They shook hands.

"Thank you, sir. Sorry if I'm a few minutes late. First train ride on your subways here." Then he blurted with nervousness, "Got a little lost."

"Yes, yes, of course," said the Dean with a look of confusion on his face. Then he hid his hands inside his coat pocket and the room fell silent for a moment.

Peter looked around.

"Moving to larger offices?"

"Well, as a matter of fact . . . Tell me, Mr. Thompson, didn't you receive the letter we sent?" he said with grave concern.

"Of course. Showed it to everybody in my town. They were all real happy for us, you know with things being tough everywhere these days," he said with understated pride.

The Dean cleared his throat, sucked on his pipe, then exhaled a long plume of smoke. "I understand, but you see . . . ," he said softly, "we sent another letter." Clearly emphasizing the word *another*.

"No . . . I didn't get that one. . . . My wife and I, we've been traveling for three weeks now. Our truck almost didn't make it . . . but as you can see . . ." And Peter smiled, tugging at his lapels.

The Dean turned away.

"Is something wrong?"

Dean Stephenson dropped his eyes, took a deep breath, bit down on his pipe, inhaled long and hard, and as he spoke, Peter felt his life being sucked right out of him. He took a step back and his legs felt weak and wobbly and the room fell dark. . . .

＊

Lucy stood in front of the small mirror on top of the little dresser and nervously fussed with her skirt and blouse. She wanted to look picture-perfect for her husband, because tonight was his night. He had worked so hard for this opportunity and she was proud of him, proud to be his wife. We've been through so much, she thought, and her mind drifted to the painful loss of their parents, then to the wrenching experience of watching their friends and neighbors lose their farms and homes after the collapse of the economy, then the sleepless nights they endured struggling to overcome their own apprehensions about giving up all that they cherished in order to move to this chaotic city and start a new life—a better life, she hoped—then she stopped herself and rephrased her thought, saying to herself now with determination, It *will* be a better life. The image of Peter came back to her, and for whatever reason, the distinctive aroma of the Old Spice cologne he splashed on his face each morning passed through the air and she was comforted, her nervousness subsiding. She felt confident that he was on track to get his degree, calculating once again that his wages would be more than adequate and that now, most importantly, with his steady income they could save in order to have the family they always wanted. A little girl, she thought. We'll name her Ellie after my mom, Ellen, and she instinctively touched her belly for the briefest of seconds, then caught herself, saying, Not yet . . . one thing at a time, let's get settled, let's have fun. It was, after all, their first night stepping out on the town and she wanted it to be lovely and carefree.

She reached for her scarf and draped it around her

neck, fluffing it up in all the right places. Don't want to get cold while riding through Central Park in those elegant hansom cabs, she thought. But then again, if she did catch a chill, she could always snuggle up to Peter and bury her head into his strong, accommodating chest. She was tempted to discard the scarf because it was so much nicer to be warmed by him, but she didn't. For the last time, she looked into the mirror, quickly ran her brush through her hair, checked her lipstick—not too much, not too little—and finally decided she was pleased with how she looked. She grabbed her coat, patted all the animals good-bye, and headed for the door, when—

BANG! BANG! BANG! Startled, Lucy watched the front door heave inward, the metal hinges straining to stay attached to the wood as the pounding outside continued. The animals squeaked and barked, chirped and croaked, then ricocheted all over the house like electrically charged pinballs, knocking over knickknacks, lamps, tables, and chairs. Then, silence, after they all found safe refuge under whatever furniture was left standing and in one piece. Lucy hesitantly cracked open the door and there she saw it: the contorted, angry face of Mrs. Hardwick looming large.

"I'm getting complaints!" she screamed and Lucy almost choked on the smell of garlic wafting out of the landlady's mouth.

She covered her nose with the palm of her hand and gently nudged past the old hag, closing the door behind her.

"I was just leaving," Lucy said, hoping this encounter was going to be brief.

"Oh, yeah . . . ?" said Hardwick. Her suspicious green eyes narrowed to slits as she took a step closer, pinning Lucy's back against the door. Trapped, Lucy froze with fright as Mrs. Hardwick's thin neck stretched up and out until her twisted face was right up to Lucy's and the poor girl's knees started to wobble and she feared she was going to faint. With her hands behind her, Lucy quickly grabbed the doorknob and held on for dear life.

"There's too much noise," Hardwick spat out. "The parrots are making a racket, that *mutt* of yours with its three idiotic names won't shut its trap, and now there's talk in the neighborhood that you and your husband are keeping some very large animals in there."

"They're just pets . . . ," said Lucy, her hand still pressed tight against her face. Then she looked down, hoping to find a black pit, a trap door, a magic potion, anything to help her disappear and avoid this rotten, evil woman, but all she saw was the pockmarked, wood planks of the floor and she was stuck.

Hardwick wasn't buying it. "Who ever heard of keeping pets during times like these? Wasting good money on things you can't eat. What kind of *saps* are you?"

Lucy stiffened. "You're not very nice—" And Lucy wanted to wring her scrawny neck, or worse, maybe kick her in her shins, but she wasn't brought up that way so she unfortunately had to dismiss those options.

"Ahhh, just keep 'em quiet and get rid of those moose or wild horses or whatever you got living in there before the Board of Health shows up and kicks us all out into the streets."

"I'll make sure to cover the parrots up each night," Lucy mumbled in a tired way.

"You better or I'm gonna raise your rent," threatened Hardwick, spewing a final, putrid wave of garlic through the air that instantly killed a fly buzzing overhead. Hardwick spun around, stormed down the stairs, and judging from all the termites that fell from the beams in the hallway, slammed her door shut with a terrific bang.

Light headed and frustrated, Lucy stood still for a moment, looked at the fly and the concussed termites on the ground, and wondered why Hardwick was so mean. She probably didn't have a family—no one to love. But why, she wondered, why would anyone who hated people with such intensity spend their life as a landlady surrounded by people? It made no sense to her. She should have been a gravedigger, Lucy reasoned. Nice solitary work with no one to argue with, and she covered her mouth, surprised by her own cynical thought. Then Dodger-the-Podger poked his head out of the door, barked softly, and Lucy was instantly reminded that she was running late.

She scooted the mutt back inside and hushed all the animals, who jabbered with relief seeing that she was still alive. Lucy ran to the bed, quickly pulled a long linen box out from under it, threw off the lid, whipped out a half dozen sheets and pillowcases, and covered all the cages and aquariums. Silence. Out of breath, she looked down and saw the expectant eyes of Montclair-Sinclair-Éclair and Dodger-the-Podger, standing side by side, wondering what Lucy was going to do with them. She dropped a blanket over them and the silly cat and dog nestled lovingly together underneath.

# FOUR

Haunted by the words of Dr. Stephenson, Peter sat on a bench in the middle of Riverside Park.

*"Two weeks ago the Board of Trustees called an emergency meeting. . . . They canceled the program."*

Peter finished his sandwich, crumpled up the wax paper. He then walked out of the park and for hours wandered aimlessly through the city streets . . .

*"I'm sorry," said the Dean. "Everything, including your position. You see, Peter, it's the Depression."*

. . . paying no attention to the ball whizzing past his head struck by a group of truant boys playing stickball (sewer to sewer) in the street . . .

*"The school has lost millions. There's simply no money left."*

. . . blind to the frantic smudge-faced firemen with ladders and hoses in their hands racing by him as they

battled the flames shooting out of an abandoned building . . .

*"We had no choice. I'm terribly sorry. I wish you the
best of luck."*

. . . not even noticing the street lamp that came
crashing down in front of him after being struck by an
old man driving a Model T Ford; he wasn't even aware
that he was now being jostled and bounced by the rush-
ing crowds of office workers marching toward the
trains, their homes, their families, their rendezvous along
Fifth Avenue . . .

*"You're a young man, Peter. I'm sure you'll find
something—I'm terribly sorry."*

. . . And it wasn't until he absentmindedly stepped
into the middle of the street and saw an old woman
pointing, silently mouthing at him, "Watch out!" that his
mind finally snapped back into consciousness and he
began to register the curious fear in her eyes. Then, and
only then, did Peter hear the piercing, screeching sounds
of a coal truck braking just seconds before impact— With
lightning speed, he whipped around, saw the truck heading right for him, its metal grille just inches from his face.
He jumped back onto the curb and the truck drove past
him with such speed his hat flew off his head. Hearing his
own heart pound, Peter knelt on one knee, took a couple
of deep breaths, and with his hands shaking like a feeble
old man, grabbed his hat off the sidewalk, stood up, and
shuffled away with the embarrassed, unsteady footsteps
of someone learning to walk for the first time.

Still in a daze, he turned off Fifth Avenue, walked down a street less traveled, and passed a small jewelry store, where his eyes caught a glimpse of himself reflected in the windowpane and he stopped in shock. He appeared older, tired-looking, the skin of his face sagging down as if there were an invisible hand behind his neck lifting him off the ground. He pressed his face closer until his nose almost touched the glass, and he stared into his own eyes now filled with fear. He took a step back, rubbed his face, and told himself to calm down. He leaned in again, looked at his reflection, touching his nose, cheeks, eyes, and felt better as everything, thankfully, began to appear more familiar.

Calmer now and desperate to forget the last few harrowing moments, he peered back into the window, allowing his eyes to roam over all sorts of watches and fobs, earrings and bracelets, all nicely laid out on a series of carpeted shelves. He was about to walk away when his eyes caught the sight of a small antique-looking crystal snowflake pendant hanging in the corner of the window display and he paused. Then, without knowing why, he pressed his hands against the glass and stared at it, and the more he focused on its delicate carving and its intricate detail, the whole pendant began to slowly twist and turn and glisten with light. Peter was riveted by its mysterious beauty and before he knew it, he had triggered a bunch of little bells swinging from the movement of the shop door as he walked inside.

The smiling, pear-shaped salesman wearing a thick

wool suit quickly wiped his sweaty brow with a hanky, leaned to one side, and rolled off his stool; then with his pudgy hands, he pulled back his jacket and proudly patted his waist, which bulged like a pie crust stuffed with too many berries. Right off the bat, Peter suspected that he was in the presence of an odd man. It wasn't just because of the salesman's round, helium-filled face, punctuated by two large, wide-open eyes that glistened with the same excitement of a five-year-old child blowing out his birthday candles; nor was it his thin wet lips, which stretched from ear to ear in a permanent, almost comical smile across his face. No, it was something else, and Peter's suspicions were confirmed immediately, when the salesman opened his little mouth and blurted out, "Good afternoon!" and Peter's jaw just about fell off its hinges. The man's voice was ludicrously high, dolphinlike, spoken in octaves a tuning fork couldn't replicate, a violin couldn't achieve, even the elves up in the North Pole would wince and plug up their ears with gingerbread—and Peter thanked his lucky stars he wasn't a dog, because if he were, he would have dropped on all fours and howled in pain. Yet Peter managed a small, polite smile while quickly trying to attribute where this abnormality came from, and he deduced it was the salesman's bow tie—wrapped so tightly around his neck it clearly constricted not only his vocal cords, but possibly the very flow of blood to his head, and Peter wanted to shout, Loosen the bow tie! but he didn't.

The salesman wiped the sweat off his brow again and

said in that high-pitched voice, "And what attracts you today, sir?"

Peter paused, allowing his ears to adjust to that sound, then said, "That necklace, the one with the snowflake on it. The one in the window display."

The salesman waddled even closer. "Oh, yes . . . Very delicate craftsmanship right there, yes, sir, real delicate," the salesman cooed, smelling a sale. "Must be for a very special lady. That snowflake is pure crystal." As if there were such a thing as fake crystal, thought Peter. It's called glass! But Peter didn't argue the point, because he was more interested in the pendant.

The salesman looked up, artfully raised his right eyebrow, leaned in close to Peter. "It's a one of a kind," he whispered, trying to tempt Peter with this privileged information. He reached into the display case, gently pulled it out, let it hang from his fingers for a few seconds, then waved it over to Peter like a magician finishing his trick.

Peter took it from his hand, studied it, then looked back at the salesman. "Unique, like the real ones."

The salesman quickly agreed.

"How much?"

"Ten dollars," the salesman answered, adding, "and that's a bargain."

Peter dipped into his pocket and the salesman's eyes opened wider. Peter pulled out a few tens and the salesman's eyes ballooned with anticipation. Peter stared at the cash and the salesman exhaled long and hard, hoping the release of oxygen and all sorts of other gases building inside him would keep his eyes from blowing out of his head. Then Peter stuffed the cash back into his pocket and the salesman's eyes shut tight with the hiss of disappointment and Peter eyed the salesman, noticing some vapors floating around the man's head.

"I'm sorry, maybe next time," Peter said with embarrassment. He turned and walked toward the door.

"Well, Christmas is coming in a few months. That is, if you change your mind . . . ," yelled the salesman, and Peter could hear the dogs all over the city barking in pain. Peter didn't respond; instead, he answered the disappointed salesman by closing the door behind him.

# FIVE

The glorious New York City Plaza Hotel sparkled under the star-filled night. Horse-drawn carriages trampling over the golden autumn leaves dropped off the wealthy elite, uniformly clad in their gowns and tuxedos. Anxious doormen quickly ushered them out of the carriages, and with an elaborate bow guided them toward the door. The privileged guests smiled, stepped ever so carefully onto the curb, then sauntered arm in arm up the stairs as if they had all the time in the world.

All dolled up, Lucy sat on a bench across the street and watched it all, dreamt of it all—imagining herself and Peter, a tuxedo for him, a gold lamé dress for her, attending a midnight ball for some Greek prince. They would drink champagne from Tiffany glasses and eat dainty caviar spread on little pieces of toast; their heads would fall back with laughter as some fabulously wealthy banker begged them for the chance to invest in Peter's new animal hospital. Then she thought about their night, where and what they would eat first—perhaps we'll take a stroll down to the Oyster Bar in Grand Central—we'll eat some oysters and split a bottle of soda. After that, we'll ride the hansom cab and not just through Central Park, but through all the boroughs, from Manhattan to Queens, from the Bronx to Brooklyn. Well, almost all of them, she thought laughing, knowing that she had left the underpopulated wastelands of Staten Island off her list. But no, she thought, I must ask him all about his day . . . and as she tried to organize her thoughts, she turned and saw an old man sitting on another bench, just across from her, throwing bread crumbs at the pigeons. Bobbing and cooing, the pigeons warily circled the man, then with a dart of their beaks, they'd snatch a crumb off the ground, then quickly scamper away. The old man threw some more crumbs and he and the pigeons started the game all over again. Lucy smiled at the old man, but he quickly averted her gaze. That was odd, she thought, and she fidgeted in her seat and looked up, anxious to see Peter. And there he was! She jumped up smiling and he came into her arms. They kissed.

"Tell me! Tell me how it went," she said excitedly.

"Like a dream," he said a little too sharply.

"And you charmed them all?"

"All smiles and laughs," he said, trying his best to mask his dour mood.

Lucy pulled him down to the bench, snuggled close,

and secretly took in his scent, smelling again his distinctive after-shave, and she smiled.

"And Dean Stephenson, he was nice? He was glad to see you?" she said.

Peter looked around, in fact, he looked everywhere else but at her. He finally mumbled from the side of his mouth, "The Dean couldn't have been more attentive."

He turned, looked across the street, and saw the rich clientele entering the Plaza. His blood boiled and he became enraged because their success and wealth reminded him of his failure and impending poverty. Then he silently cursed himself for having such a self-pitying thought.

"And what about your office? I bet it's nice and large," she said innocently, holding his arm tighter.

"You bet, doll," he said quickly. "It's the biggest thing I've ever . . . bigger than the Plaza itself," and he pulled his jacket tight around his neck.

Lucy was overcome with joy. "Oh, Peter," she sighed, and she nestled deeper into his chest, burying her head in his wool jacket, which drove him nearly out of his mind because for the first time in his life, he couldn't reciprocate her affections. He loved her more than ever, and if he could, he would have reached out and held her, grabbed her tight, swallowed her whole, but he didn't because he felt like a miserable failure, felt personally responsible for killing their dreams, and worse, he felt like a fraud, unworthy of giving or accepting any love. He was scared. He was trapped. He had to tell her. But how? He couldn't think straight. Everything was in a jumble. Words, phrases, whole sentences, ran through his head, but he couldn't string them together in any cogent, fluid thought, and as he struggled for the right words, his eyes wandered over to the old man sitting on the bench across from them and he became agitated.

"Look at that guy—"

And sure enough, the old man was luring a few more pigeons toward him.

Lucy looked up. "He's just an old man," she said gently, tugging at his arm. "Come on, let's hop on a buggy."

But Peter pulled back. "No. Wait. What's he doing!?"

A pigeon was circling closer.

"Come on, Peter, let's go."

He wouldn't move. Instead, he watched the old man lure another pigeon closer, closer still, until the scavenging bird was right next to the old man's torn leather shoes and then WHAM—the old man whipped a pillowcase over the bird, and before anyone knew it, the captured bird was jammed inside the old man's coat pocket.

Furious, Peter jumped up. "HEY! You can't do that! LET THE BIRD GO!"

The frightened old man looked up, saw Peter, and then quickly pulled his fedora down over his eyes and shamefully scurried away.

"HEY!" Peter screamed again. "Get back here!" Peter took a couple of quick steps toward him, but Lucy jumped up, grabbed his arm. "Leave him be, Peter. He has to eat," she said with tender empathy.

"But that's crazy!" he said, filled with rage.

"No, it's not. We're just lucky," she said soothingly.

Peter turned, looked at her, and said sarcastically, "Yeah . . . we're lucky."

Lucy studied his eyes. "What's the matter? What happened today?"

Peter sat dejectedly back down on the bench, took a deep breath, then gently lifted her hands in his. "Honey, I've something to tell you."

"I know."

"Lucy . . ." And he paused.

She reached for him.

"Honey . . . there *is* no job," he said haltingly, and for a brief second, Lucy was stunned.

"It wasn't anything we did—" he said, and Lucy quickly cut him off.

"I'm sure," she said, trying to encourage him to talk.

"They wanted me, they really did."

"I know that, my love." And with her forgiving eyes, she searched his face and Peter slowly felt a change come over him. Her understanding and acceptance of him filled his heart with strength and all his self-pitying thoughts began to dissipate. He knew, then, that together they would somehow get through this momentary setback.

"It's the Depression," he explained while gently rubbing her hand. "They canceled the entire program, everything, not just my job."

Lucy leaned in and kissed his cheek. "It's okay, honey."

As they stared silently into each other's eyes, not

knowing what to say next, not yet trusting their emotions, the cold autumn wind blew hard, scattering the leaves like whirlpools around them, and they felt a chill.

"So how long can we last?" Lucy finally asked with concern.

"If we sell the truck and we're careful, a couple of months."

"It's all our savings."

"I know. I guess this is that rainy day we always hear people talking about."

"But now we're those people," Lucy said sadly, and they looked at each other, both recalling the indelible images they saw when they first drove through the streets of New York: the desperate vendors warming their hands, the poor digging into their pockets for a few pennies, the little children grabbing hunks of coal off the street, the withered old man selling a bent and rusted fork.

Yet, Peter was determined to overcome their predicament, so he quickly erased these thoughts and said with all the confidence he could muster, "Not for long, my love. Not for long. I promise."

Holding hands, they stood and looked at the hansom cabs gliding elegantly past them. They put their heads down and began their slow, silent walk back home.

## SIX

Three months passed and Peter still couldn't find a job, but that didn't stop him from getting up each morning, dutifully circling the want ads in the *Herald Tribune,* then with a sandwich that Lucy made for him jammed into his coat pocket, he would walk the city streets, occasionally interviewing, but most often just walking, hoping to see a sign hanging from a store, a factory, any place of business looking for help. But no such luck, because the cold facts were these: There was no work to be had, and even though Peter was bright and educated, he was still, after all, a veterinarian in training, and in times like this, animals were hardly a priority (even the police were replacing their horses with cars), and worse, he wasn't a skilled laborer, so even bricklaying jobs were out of the question. Yet he never stopped believing that, yessiree Bob, today was the day he was going to find work, and he would give Lucy a big ol' juicy kiss on her forehead, pat all the animals good-bye, and race out the door expecting to find that pot of gold in this Christmas season.

Salvation Army "Santas" stood on every corner ringing their bells and shouting, "Ho, ho, ho," waiting, hoping to hear the precious "ping" of a coin or two dropping inside their iron pots. But for the first time in recent memory these Santas outnumbered the few shoppers, who all turned a deaf ear to the ringing appeals for charity because they were too busy looking for bargains. Yet the Santas persisted and they shook their bells with increased determination and vigor, but all they did was cast an unfortunate pall over the already depressed spirits of these New Yorkers. So their bells, along with the Christmas decorations that hung from every street lamp, every storefront, off every hook and nail, were now just painful reminders to the good people of New York that they couldn't rummage together enough change to buy something for their loved ones, let alone help their fellow man in this season of giving. The Salvation Army pots lay silent and empty.

Tired and hungry, Peter pressed on, but each store he passed posted this sign: "NOT HIRING." Undeterred, he headed down another block and came upon one of those unique little fenced-in parks found in the most unusual parts of the city, now filled with scrawny little Christmas trees for sale. He leaned against the chain link and watched the little children, followed by their protective parents, run excitedly around pointing, tugging, trying to pick the perfect tree to bring home for Santa. It had to be perfect they thought. If Santa wasn't pleased with their choice, he might not leave all the gifts they wanted.

✳

The apartment was in chaos. Rodger-Dodger-the-Podger chased Montclair-Sinclair-Éclair, who jumped onto the drapes and clawed her way to the top of the windowsill— the turtles, the parrots, the marsupials and crickets all carried on, jabbering, chirping, squeaking like mad as if they were in the midst of deciding the very fate of their animal kingdom. Meanwhile, Lucy was perspiring as she hovered over the stove, stirring soup. She reached for the salt, but there was none. The cupboards were almost bare. Annoyed, she whipped around and hushed all the animals quiet, but her appeals went unanswered as the animals continued arguing amongst themselves.

Frustrated and edgy, she wiped the hair from her face, then suddenly felt faint and her knees buckled. She grabbed the ledge of the kitchen sink and held on, took a couple of deep breaths, ran the water, and rinsed her face with her shaking hands. What's wrong with me— perhaps I'm not eating enough, she thought, when suddenly the front door burst open and there was Peter struggling with a Christmas tree that was clearly way too large for the room. Lucy quickly regained her composure and dried her hands on her apron.

"What, did you rob Rockefeller Center? Are you crazy?"

"It's Christmas time, sweetie," said Peter excitedly as he put the tree down.

"But we don't have any money," she protested.

"Don't worry. I have a feeling something's going to come our way soon."

"Peter, two weeks from now, Mrs. Hardwick is going to be knocking on our door demanding rent, and in a month's time, we'll be on the breadlines like everyone else. What then?"

Peter lifted the tree and it swayed in the air, almost knocking over a few aquariums. All the animals quickly jumped up and squawked nervously. "Sweetheart, this is the season for good luck. You just have to believe," he said out of breath.

"In luck or Christmas?" she said wryly.

"In Christmas, you lunkhead. You believe in that, everything else falls into place."

"You're definitely not eating enough," warned Lucy.

"And neither are you, but you watch. Now that we have this tree, something good is going to happen to us," he said assuredly. Then with a surge of energy, he righted the tree, propped it up in the corner of the room, clapped his hands together, and faced Lucy with a look of great accomplishment.

"And you know what else?"

"What now?"

He stood straight and firm. "If you believe in Christmas and Santa, truly believe in them . . ."

Lucy eyed him suspiciously. "Go on . . ."

"Then when you die . . ."

"God forbid . . . ," she interrupted.

"That's right, God forbid, but when you die, you can choose where you want to go: Heaven or the North Pole," he said confidently.

"Really?"

"Really and absolutely. You have a choice," he said smiling.

But Lucy wasn't smiling. A look of grave concern crossed her face. "You need a job," she said, and Peter laughed. "Because no one has a choice," she continued. "And besides, there are no people in the North Pole. There are only elves up there—those weird-looking little people with big pointy ears."

"Nosiree Bob," he said with certainty. "There are elves up there, I agree. Plenty of them. But there's all sorts of regular people up there too, like me and you. Young ones, old ones, cobblers, tailors, teachers, and paupers, anybody that believes in Santa. It's a great way to spend eternity. You get to play with the reindeer and make toys for the kids."

"And who filled your ears up with all this nonsense?"

Peter paused, looked long and hard at his wife, then said truthfully, "My mother. She told me that right before she died." He paused, then softly added, "And I believed her."

Lucy shook her head in wonder and amazement at his boyish, contagious charm. She slowly walked over to him, fell into his open arms, kissed him, and their lips barely parted for the remainder of the evening.

## SEVEN

The elderly doctor dropped his instruments into the white metal canister boiling with steam and water. He slammed the lid shut, adjusted his stethoscope, and turned to Lucy, who was quickly buttoning up her blouse as she sat on the examining table. He cleared his throat and Lucy looked up nervously.

"Well, you definitely have something," he said evenly.

And Lucy's heart sank. "What is it?" she asked tensely.

"I'm not sure." But as he said this, his lips started to curl, revealing a small, almost coy smile. "Could go both ways."

"Am I . . . ?"

"You sure are," said the doctor, beaming.

"Oh, my God. When?" she asked, placing her hands on her cheeks and feeling the blood rush to her face.

"If my math is correct, next July. Merry Christmas," he said pleasantly.

Lucy slowly climbed off the table and hugged the doctor with all her strength, not wanting to let go, not wanting him to see the small tear falling from her eye. She wiped it away, wondering how she was going to tell Peter.

✳

It was Christmas Eve night and the stores were closing early, but despite the constant rejection, Peter refused to give up his hunt for a job. He had promised himself that he would get one by Christmas day and *that* was now only hours away. He had to find some work, and besides, what better Christmas gift could he give to Lucy than some desperately needed hope and security? She deserves that, he thought. She deserves everything. He fixed his hat and tie, marched down another factory-lined street, crossed directly in front of a hansom cab stable, and BAM! Peter was knocked down by a wild-eyed horse that came lurching out of the barn; and following right behind the horse was the short and scruffy, cigar-smoking, sixty-year-old black owner, yelling in a raspy voice, "Whoah! Whoah! HOLD ON THERE! Whoah!" but the more the old man yelled, the more the horse kicked and reared; so the salty old man decided to wave his arms like a rodeo clown, hoping to distract the crazy, out-of-control animal from trampling over Peter, who was still on the ground writhing in pain.

"Get up, friend, get up, pal!" the old man shouted as he vainly jumped up and down trying to grab hold of the horse's reins. But Peter stayed on the ground groaning, his hands scraping along the sidewalk, hoping to find his senses, which, he was sure, were scattered like marbles all over the pavement.

"GET UP!" the old man pleaded again.

Peter finally looked up and saw the horse's hooves coming down over his head. He quickly rolled out of the way, and in one fluid move, leapt back to his feet and grabbed hold of the reins.

"Whoah! OKAY, CALM DOWN, BOY! THAT'S IT," Peter yelled, and after a few more minutes of being knocked silly, Peter managed to bring the animal under control.

"This way, this way," the old man said, beckoning. Still dazed, Peter dragged the horse back into the stable, where he locked the animal up inside the stall. Exhausted and shaking, Peter and the old man took a couple of deep breaths, then looked at each other.

"I coulda done that myself, yessiree, coulda done that myself, was just about to get him under control, too, when you came along, but whoozawhatztaknow! So, thanks, because I appreciate that little help," said the old man as if Peter were just a mere bystander and had done nothing more than light the old man's cigar. Is everyone crazy in this city? Peter thought. I just risked my life, almost got mauled, almost had my brains bashed in, and this old man thinks nothing out of the usual happened.

"It's okay," said Peter, readjusting all his clothes.

The old man extended his hand. "The name's George."

"Peter." They shook. "What's wrong with him?" Peter said pointing to the horse, who was now spinning in circles inside his stall.

"Whoozawhatztaknow, that's what I wants to know. I was putting a new shoe on him and he shot outta here likes a stallion in those derbies I listens to on the radio from time to time. I take care of him . . . sure do . . . feed him real good . . . sure do . . . keep him warm . . . sure do, do all that too . . . but whoozawhatztaknow. That's what I say." And he sucked hard on his stogie.

"Mind if I take a look?" said Peter.

"Be my guest. Just don't get yourself killed, likes you almost did before. But thanks the Lord I was around, otherwise whoozawhatztaknow might have happened," said the old man, waving his cigar with a flourish in the air.

Peter looked at him and said, "You're right. I'll be careful, and thanks again for saving my life."

"Don't mention it," said the old man proudly.

Peter walked into the stable and gently patted the horse on his rump until the horse stopped spinning. He reached down and pulled up the horse's hind hoof and examined it closely, touching it in specific places, until the horse let out a small plaintive whinny and Peter let it drop back onto the hay covering the floor.

"He's got calcium deposits," Peter said expertly, stroking the horse's mane with his hand. "That hurts bad. You have to saw them off."

George looked at him curiously. "How do ya know that?! Whattaya work with animals? Read some books or something?"

"Was going to be a vet."

"Oh, yeah . . ." And George blew out a plume of smoke, looked him up and down. "You need a job?"

"Who doesn't?" Peter quickly responded.

"My last guy took to the bottle. I need a driver and somebody to help me keep my horses fit and uh . . . whoozawhatztaknow what else."

"That's why I'm here," Peter said with excitement. "What are you paying?"

George chomped on his stogie for a few seconds, spit a small wet piece of the brown leaf off his lip. "Ten bucks a week, plus—" And he chomped on his cigar for another minute or two. "Plus tips . . . ?" he added almost apologetically.

Peter couldn't believe his ears. "You got a deal!"

"But you starts right now. There's a tux hanging inside. It's a little worn, there's a hole in the knee, the cuffs are all frayed, and the jacket's got some stains all over from who knows where, but all in all it's a dandy and it should fit ya."

"Right now?!" Peter asked in shock. "You see, tonight's Christmas Eve and my wife is expecting me home any second for dinner . . . I can start tomorrow."

"I *know* what tonight is and *believe me,* the Mrs. will understand," George said knowingly.

But Peter knew he was right. A job is a job, and right now, the job was most important. Lucy will understand, he thought. Of course she'll understand. She'll more than understand. She's going to jump up and down. I can't wait to see her. Hot diggitty dog, I got a job! he wanted to scream, but instead he looked at George and said coolly, "Fair enough. But I have one small favor to ask."

"Yeah and . . . ?" said George.

"I need an advance."

George looked him in the eyes. Chomped a bit more on his stogie. "Couple of bucks do you?"

"I need the ten."

George chomped on his stogie like it was a carrot, stared Peter in the eyes, wondering if this guy was trustworthy. Peter smiled and George swallowed his cigar, let out a small little burp, and said, "I trust ya, but then again, whoozawhatztaknow who you can trust these days . . ."

And with that, George reached deep into his pocket, pulled out a wrinkled ten-spot, and handed it to Peter, who grabbed it, spun on his heels, and ran for the door screaming, "THANK YOU, THANK YOU!"

"HURRY UP NOW! I GOT A LOTS TO DO. SANTA MAY COME BY THIS EVENING."

Peter stopped dead in his tracks. "What . . . ?!" he said, touching his ears, thinking he definitely damaged them in the fall.

"Santa," George said again, as if that were the most natural name to roll off his or anyone else's lips. Peter stood still and listened.

"Let me tell you something. . . . Maybe you know this and maybe you don't, but I gotta feeling *you'll* understand. . . . Sometimes things happen to the reindeer. Their reins snap or a shoe falls off and I helps them out. But I got to tell you, I never saw none of those calcium deposits on their feets. That's a new one for me, but whoozawhatztaknow, it may happen this year. So hurry up back. I don't want to disappoint him."

## EIGHT

Oblivious to the crowds, Lucy raced through the streets, stopping in front of a children's shop. She peered into the window and saw a small, delicately carved wooden rattle. She looked at the en-trance and saw the owner flipping over the "CLOSED" sign on the door. Lucy quickly tapped on the glass, pointed to the rattle, clasped her hands in desperation in front of her lips, saying, "Please . . ." The owner paused, looked at her, then at his watch, then unlocked the door and Lucy charged in.

Wearing his top hat and dressed in his ill-fitting tuxedo, Peter sat high and proud on his driver's perch, gingerly guiding his old horse and hansom cab through the con-gested streets of the city, expertly nudging "Old Henry" past cars and trucks and the hundreds of people running to get home for Christmas Eve. The excitement of Christmas was in the air and with his new job, Peter felt like a million bucks. In fact, he could hardly contain himself. Heck, why don't I just let this old horse gallop downtown, stop in front of Hardwick's place, and yell up to Lucy: We did it! We did it! Nah, I can't do that. And he smiled, knowing he had not one, but *two* surprises for her, and he gently patted his coat pocket. Best ten bucks I ever spent, he thought. But it will have to wait. Better to make a few more quarters in tips, maybe even buy her a small bouquet of flowers on the way home. Then, dreaming about falling into her arms, he saw a lovely young couple on the corner excitedly wave to him, and Peter pulled his horse over. Smiling, the couple quickly jumped aboard.

Peter whipped around and said, "Good evening!" Then with great theatrical flair, he unfurled a beautiful plaid quilt and draped it over their knees. The couple was both shocked and charmed by his unexpected gallantry and for a second they doubted they were really in New York. But Peter knew better. He knew that all New Yorkers (well, most, at least) were truly misunderstood, because he himself was now one.

"So where would you like Old Henry to go?" Peter said, patting the horse's neck. The couple smiled, then pulled the quilt high up to their necks and started talking excitedly to each other: "How about around the Waldorf?"—"No, honey, let's see the Empire State

Building!"—"No, no, no, take us downtown . . . up-town!"—"Take us all the way back to Kansas . . ." And they all laughed.

❄

Back at home, Lucy put the finishing touches on a nicely laid-out dinner on their small kitchen table, took a step back, and saw: a piping hot roast beef surrounded by baked potatoes, a golden roast goose with apple raisin dressing, a rum-soaked ham plugged with hundreds of cloves, a bowl of butternut squash with just the right dash of cinnamon sprinkled over it, a mincemeat-pear pie (that she was especially proud of), a large fruitcake, some gingerbread cookies, and at the far end of the table, a zesty plum pudding. She then blinked and smiled at: the tiny little chicken with two small potatoes rolling around on the oversized plate in the middle of the table. It wasn't much, but she was glad to have scraped together enough change to buy it. She looked at her watch again and noticed it was getting late. She lit the candles and then placed the wrapped rattle next to Peter's plate, sat down, and waited, wondering where her husband was.

❄

"Pay attention to where you're going! We're late and your father's going to be mad! You know how important his Christmas Eve dinner is!" screamed the nervous and impatient mother as she spun back around and saw her little ten-year-old son still standing on the sidewalk next to the Plaza Hotel. Furious, she twirled her black pocketbook like a medieval sling, charged back to the curb, and just before the little boy got brained by the bag, he ducked, but she grabbed his little paw and yanked him into the street, almost pulling his arm out of his socket. "WHAT ARE YOU LOOKING AT? JUST WAIT UNTIL I GET YOU HOME. NO CHRISTMAS PIE FOR YOU!" she screamed.

The little boy shrugged her off, because what he was seeing was certainly more fascinating and definitely more fulfilling than any of his mother's overly sweet Christmas pies which she always stuffed with those horrible little teeth breaking candies. Who needs it—the pie stinks, he wanted to say, and he had been wanting to say that to her ever since he was old enough to talk which was eight long years ago. But fearing her hand, he kept quiet and remained still, staring in wonder at all the people, the traffic, the lights. This was great. This was life. "OUCH, THAT HURTS!" he cried as his mother grabbed him by the ears—and the next thing he knew, he was being dragged across the street like a vaudeville act getting the hook.

Peter snuck a quick look at the couple sitting all snuggled up and warm in the back. "What a beautiful night. Just look at all those stars," he said pleasantly.

"It's magic," said the young lady, marveling at the sky.

"Sure is," said Peter. "New York's the greatest place in the world. And I'll tell you what—If you look closely you might even see a shooting star and that means—"

"What?" interrupted the girl excitedly.

"It means someone has decided to go live with Santa up in the North Pole. That's how you get there. A shooting star."

He turned back around and saw the puzzled looks on their faces.

"Oh, yeah, it's true," he continued. "But that's okay, my wife doesn't believe me either."

The couple smiled weakly, then nodded politely, and the wife secretly squeezed her husband's hand as if to say, Stay quiet. Peter spun back around and smiled as he guided Old Henry down the street.

The obnoxious mother sucked on her teeth and tapped her black high heels on the curb while she waited for the light to change. Green! And she, along with the crowds, charged across the street. She was about to step onto the sidewalk when she realized that, once again, her son had wriggled free of her claws and was now standing alone in the middle of the street, pointing up to the sky.

"Look!" the boy said with wonder as his eyes followed a brilliant shooting star blazing across the Manhattan skyline. Then without any warning, the heavens above him exploded in a brilliant meteor shower, and thousands, then millions, of shooting stars flew in every direction, zipping from left to right, right to left, darting up and down, leaving streams of white light etched permanently against the black sky.

Peter saw it too, and he rose to his feet and exclaimed, "SEE! SEE THAT! Wow, the North Pole must be hopping!" His enthusiasm was so infectious, the couple immediately strained their necks to the sky, but as hard as they tried, they didn't see anything.

Suddenly, there was another burst of brilliant light and to Peter and the young boy, it appeared as if God's own hand cut the solar systems loose and trillions of stars fell from the heavens with a relentless but elegant fury; and slowly, the very street they were on, the hotels and the office buildings, all the dark alleys snaking through the city—indeed, the whole wide world—seemed to light up. The little boy and Peter shielded their eyes from the strobing images of the shooting stars gracing them with light. Then two more massive stars collided above them, and they felt their hearts almost burst with joy as millions of shards of flickering lights sprinkled and floated down, coming closer, closer . . . The little boy raised his hands toward the heavens, hoping to catch the little lights. His fingertips were now almost within reach, when suddenly, magically, the particles of light turned to . . . snowflakes; and it began to snow heavily, steadily, blanketing everything in *his world* in a beautiful soft whiteness. The boy stuck out his tongue, and the cool snowflakes landed on its tip. It's beautiful, they whispered to themselves, but their excitement and joy was short-lived, as the loud honks of a truck caused Old Henry to whinny and buck and Peter's smile quickly changed to a look of horror as he saw the truck heading straight for the little boy.

"Johnny!" his mother screamed.

The boy turned and froze in fright. The truck was about to hit him—its brakes squeaking and straining to stop in time. Peter yelled, "NO!!!!!" and he leapt off the cab and dove for the little boy, knocking him safely out of the way of the oncoming truck and into the arms of his mother. The truck kept coming, slipping and sliding out of control on the wet snow—left, right, spinning this way, then that, the driver frantically turning the wheel. Peter scrambled to his feet, and the last thing he saw was the driver's desperate and sorry eyes through the windshield. Everyone screamed.

The driver jumped out of his truck and ran to Peter, who now lay motionless on the ground. The driver leaned down, put his ear to Peter's mouth, and waited to hear a breath. He heard one, then another. They were faint, but there was enough life left for the driver to jump back up waving his arms and yelling for help.

A couple of policemen quickly ran over and one of the officers gently moved the distraught driver away, while the other crouched down next to Peter. With great difficulty, Peter lifted his head and the policeman leaned in close. Peter whispered a few words into the policeman's ear, then his lips stopped moving and his head fell gently back.

❄

Inside their apartment, all the animals were sound asleep. Lucy picked up the uneaten little chicken and placed it back into the icebox. Dejectedly, she sat back down at the table and toyed with the wrapped rattle. There must be a good reason, she thought. Maybe he found a job and didn't have time to get home to tell me. As she sat thinking about the future, his new job, and their little baby, there was a sudden knock on the door. "Be right there, dear."

She quickly got up, patted down her dress, brushed her hair back with her hands, and called, "Coming, dear . . . ," relit the candles, pulled the chicken back out of the icebox. "Just a sec more . . . ," she said, and it wasn't until she made sure that everything was back in place for his surprise that she raced to the door. She whipped it open and faced two New York City police officers.

"Mrs. Lucy Thompson?"

"Yes . . ."

They paused, then she watched both men solemnly take off their caps, and she knew. She started to cry, slowly at first, then in deep, heart-wrenching sobs until she collapsed inside the door frame. One of the officers leaned down, comforted her as best he could, then handed her a small package wrapped in pink tissue paper.

"Ma'am, your husband asked me to give this to you. . . ."

He unwrapped it for her, and placed the crystal snowflake pendant in her hand.

"I'm so sorry," he said softly.

## NINE

The New York sky was now dark and bleak. The meteor shower was over. The snow had stopped falling and all was still and silent. The curious onlookers standing over Peter had been roped off. An ambulance was nearby and its back doors were open. Two medics leaned down, gently placed Peter onto a stretcher, and covered him from head to toe in a white sheet. The little boy he had saved stood off to the side and wiped the tears from his eyes. Even his once harried mother stood patiently by her son, firmly holding his hand.

As the medics leaned down to grab the wooden handles of the stretcher, the little boy suddenly saw a small, funnel-like flurry of snowflakes hovering over Peter's body. Mesmerized, his arm slowly rose and his little finger pointed at the snowflakes spinning faster and faster.

"Look, Mom," he said with wonder in his voice.

And the mother leaned down and said gently, "What is it, dear?"

The boy couldn't explain it or describe it. He just saw it and all he could do was whisper, "Look . . . look . . ." He fell silent as he watched the snowflakes turn into sparkling little lights now uncontrollably spinning in circles. The mother looked over to where he was pointing and saw nothing. She glanced back at her son, who remained still, and she felt her breath flutter as she saw his face glow with the same peaceful innocence of a baby having its first pleasant dream. She felt her son squeeze her hand tighter than ever before, and she said nothing.

The boy looked up and saw the lights spinning like a whirlpool until it all merged into a solitary ball of white light, rising upward, ascending higher and higher. As the boy strained his neck toward the heavens, the ball catapulted through the atmosphere—it was now a star—a shooting star moving with incredible speed, rising higher, until the earth, in all its majestic glory, vanished fast underneath it and it kept going, rocketing faster, higher—hurling past the moon, the planets, Neptune, Jupiter, Pluto, speeding through the heavens—the Milky Way and the galaxies, faster, faster—screeching toward a wall of whiteness and bursting with a BANG through a series of thick, heavy white clouds until it crashed in a fiery explosion on a stark white landscape that reached as far as the eye could see.

The smoke parted and Peter lay alone on the white, cloudy surface.

Not knowing where he was, or how he got there, he slowly stood up. He was confused, but one thing was sure, he knew he had traveled *somewhere* and he knew he got *wherever he was* pretty darn quick. He was in the middle of a vast white nothingness. He turned around and was startled to see a post rising magically out of the cloud with two signs curiously pointing in opposite directions. One read: "Heaven," and the other read: "The North Pole." He took a moment, smiled, then whispered, "My mother was right."

He walked in the direction of the North Pole and disappeared into the enveloping whiteness. At first he thought he was walking on faint clouds, but as he continued his journey, he began to hear a curious crack after each and every footstep. Not only that, he could now see his own breath and, suddenly, he realized he was actually walking across the cold, frozen tundra of the North Pole.

As he continued walking, he suddenly saw a figure. He squinted and through the milky haze, he saw a regular United States Post Office worker hunched over, pulling thousands of letters out of a sack and magically fitting them into a traditional-looking mailbox that rose out of nowhere in the middle of the frozen ground. Peter walked closer, but the mailman paid no attention to him, but Peter was now close enough to see on top of the mailbox a large sign, written in beautiful calligraphy. It read:

*Mr. and Mrs. Santa Claus*

*Kris Kringle*

*St. Nick*

*Father Christmas*

*Père Noël*

*Sinterklass*

The mailman finished stuffing the envelopes into the mailbox, walked away with his empty sack, plopped it into his official three-wheeled pushcart, tipped his hat to Peter, walked past him, and slowly disappeared into the frozen tundra. Amazed, Peter reached inside the box, pulled out a few letters, and noticed they were all written in a child's hand and every one of them was addressed to "Santa" or "Kris Kringle" . . . "The North Pole."

He smiled, put the envelopes back, and turned around, only to be startled by the sight of four large seals (the Christmas seals and protectors of the North Pole). "They weren't there a second ago," he said with certainty. Nevertheless, there they were, lounging on the frozen tundra. Peter stared at them and they exchanged looks until the trance was finally broken when the seals lifted their snouts into the air and began barking, clapping their fins louder and louder, compelling Peter for whatever reason to approach them. And as he did, they barked and clapped with such a resounding loudness all the heavens must have heard, and just as he was upon them, Santa's house began to magically appear.

Peter froze.

It was beautiful, with a large red front door covered with a big green wreath and lots of little windows with frostbitten edges framed by strands of mistletoe and a massive chimney stack on top billowing white smoke.

Peter approached the door, and just as he was about to knock, the door swung open, a hand reached out and grabbed his lapel, and he was whipped inside quicker than he could say, "Hey . . . !" The door slammed shut behind him, the house disappeared, and the seals went back to sleep on the frozen tundra.

Stunned, Peter looked around a massive room filled with people, old ones, young ones, wearing Turkish turbans, Indian sarongs, Russian fur hats, French berets, English bowler hats, Japanese kimonos, brightly colored dashikis, and muumuus with freshly cut flowers in their hair. He then noticed, working side by side with these regular people, all the elves—hundreds of them. It's magical, he thought, as he watched the fleet-footed elves pulling toys off a moving ramp that seemed to come out of the mouths of oversized brick ovens. So that's how they do it, Peter realized. The toys are cooked up! And he smiled at the ingenuity of it all.

Still in a daze, he scanned the room and saw more elves and regulars inventing new toys at their work tables, while others shoveled gifts into a couple of red sacks. Afraid to move a muscle for fear the dream would end—*And this is most definitely a dream,* he thought—he moved just his eyes, following a train track around the perimeter of the room. Then he heard the sound of a train whistle. Peter blinked and there he was: Santa himself, sitting on top of the small locomotive, waving to everyone as he went around and around! Peter smiled in vindication, now convinced this was, in fact, a dream, until he felt a playful slap on his back and heard a loud voice, with a thick, heavy Brooklyn accent, ask, "So . . . have you ever?"

Peter looked over and stared at the man who had pulled him inside. He was stocky, crusty, clad in a work shirt and suspenders, and judging by his messy gray hair, Peter figured he was at least sixty-five years old. And hearing him ask, "So, tell me already . . . what do you think?" in that distinctive voice laced with the slightest touch of impatience, Peter knew the man was definitely from New York. Yet, what impressed Peter the most was the man's eyes. They twinkled as if he were smiling and winking, except there was no wink, just the twinkle, and Peter wondered if that was the look of having found peace and happiness.

An elbow nudged Peter in his side.

"Well?"

Peter finally spoke. "It's magnificent."

"And let me tell you, this is a big operation. Very big. I'm Harry," the man said, shoving his hand with great fanfare toward Peter, expecting a hearty shake.

"Peter, Peter Thompson," he answered, and they quickly shook hands and Peter immediately turned his attention back to all the chaotic activity taking place in front of him.

"How was the ride?" asked Harry.

"Good, I guess. I'm not sure, I think I rode on a shooting star or something," Peter said without looking back.

"Yup. Shooting stars are good, comets bad," Harry said as he jammed a fist into his mouth, jerked his knee into the air, and feigned great pain, because he knew he shouldn't have said that.

"What's that?" Peter finally asked.

"Ahhh, don't worry about it," replied Harry thankfully.

Peter stood thinking, And I thought *New York* was wild. He finally faced Harry and said, "You mind if I ask you something?"

"Do I look like I would mind? Go ahead. What's roaming around in that igloo head of yours?" Harry said, quickly and pleasantly.

"The elves, I always wanted to know—"

"Elves, schmelves," Harry said, interrupting with a wave of his hand. "But hey, don't get me wrong, they're good people. I *like* them—hard workers too. But if you're looking for creativity—" and he tapped his fingers on his forehead "—you need *life* experiences, and that's where people like you and me come in. You think it's easy coming up with new toys every year?" he said knowingly, expecting Peter to quickly agree.

Peter didn't respond.

"Hey," said Harry. "Did you hear me?"

"Remarkable" was all that came out of Peter's mouth.

"You make toys?" Harry asked and, again, Peter didn't answer and Harry was about to snap his suspenders into Peter's ears; but having gone through this routine thousands of times before, he decided to be patient and instead he said, "Whattaya got, some snow in your ears?" He paused, sucked in his stomach, then yelled right into Peter's ear: "I said, WHAT'S YOUR TRADE!?"

"Oh, uh, animals," Peter replied, sticking his forefinger into his ear and wiggling it.

That's better, thought Harry. This kid's coming around. He slapped Peter on the back and said, "Oh, yeah . . . Santa's gonna like that." Then he leaned in closer and whispered, "Because between you and me, it's a big problem. Those reindeer are real large, and the elves, well, don't smash my head with an icicle for saying this, but they're *small*. Nothing wrong with that, of course, but it's hard for them to change the reindeer's shoes, carry those big buckets of food. *You know* what I'm saying."

And just then, Santa flew by on his locomotive and waved hello. Harry noticed Peter staring at Santa, so he gently nudged him again in the ribs and said, "What can I say? He's a kid at heart, but he's the boss. Come on, we've got to get you fixed up." But before they could take one step forward, the smiling Mrs. Claus appeared in front of them.

"So nice to have you," she said sweetly.

Peter knew right off the bat that this was Mrs. Claus. He wanted to hug her with all his might, because, well he didn't really know why. She just looked like she should be hugged. She was healthy-looking and comfortably plump —plump enough to make him feel secure and protected. Her beautiful hair, brushed neatly back, was whiter than eggshells, and her soft cheeks glowed with a blushing hue of red. As with Harry, Peter was struck by her eyes, which were more than considerate; they were benevolent and alive. Peter felt himself falling into them and wanting now more than ever to hug her. He waited for her to extend her hand first, which is, of course, the gentlemanly thing to do when meeting a lady, and she did. He took her hand softly and said nervously, "How do you do?" Then he lifted her hand to his mouth and kissed it.

Mrs. Claus blushed.

"Fine, just fine, thank you. And I appreciate your gallantry. I'm Charlotte. Charlotte Claus," she added graciously.

Peter was bewildered.

"Don't look so shocked, I have a first name just like everyone else," she said sweetly.

"I didn't . . ."

"I really must do something about that," said Charlotte Claus to Harry. "The children must be getting the wrong idea."

"Ah, don't worry about it, Mrs.," interrupted Harry. "Everyone knows who's the real boss."

"See what I mean?" she said, winking at Peter, who nodded. "You must be awfully cold. Would you like some hot cocoa?"

"Give him some eggnog!" shouted Santa from a distance. And just then Santa Claus jumped off the train, came right at Peter, and gave him a great big bear hug, but this was a much different type of hug than Peter was thinking about giving Mrs. Claus. *Her* feet would never have left the ground and *her* face would never have turned blue from being squeezed so hard, but, hey, how often does one get squeezed by Santa himself? Peter actually came to enjoy it and he screamed out in happiness, "Ho . . . ho . . . hooooo!"

Santa smiled, dropped him down, looked him over approvingly, and shouted, "We should all have some eggnog! And, Harry, my friend, throw in some brandy to keep us all snug and warm!"

"It's a work night, Santa," said Harry with a definite hint of admonishment, and Peter was shocked. He never imagined anyone talking to Santa like that, but then again, it was Christmas Eve and Santa would be flying soon, and drinking and flying was never a good idea. Maybe Harry had a point. Everyone paused and Peter was filled with nervous apprehension, wondering how Santa was going to react. He was pleasantly surprised when Santa smiled broadly, slapped Harry on the back, and shouted good-naturedly, "That's right! I knew I was up to my beard with things to do!"

He faced Peter. "Well, nice to meet you, but I have to get going. . . ." He charged back into the room, full of energy and enthusiasm, then stopped, spun back around, and said with genuine interest, "By the way, you make toys?"

"Animals are my game."

"Great. We need a good man around here to take care of the reindeer."

"Told you," whispered Harry to Peter.

Then Harry looked at his watch and said with urgency, "Santa, we really should get going. You only have six minutes."

"Six minutes!" Santa exclaimed. "Why didn't you say something!?"

Harry rolled his eyes then looked at Peter with one of those "What's he think I've been talking to him about all year long" types of expressions.

Then Santa threw up his arms and yelled with excitement, "What are we all standing around for? Okay, let's move. Let's move it! Nutter, let's get those bags ready."

"I'm moving, sir. Moving as fast as I can," said the cute black elf, who immediately started shoveling thousands of toys into Santa's red sack. Amazingly, Peter noticed, the sack never appeared to fill up.

"FIVE MINUTES, EVERYONE!" shouted Harry.

Alarm bells and sirens went off! Suddenly, it was madness. Elves and the regulars pulled toys off the movable ramps, and in the back, Nutter and a few more elves shoveled more gifts into more red sacks.

Santa looked back at Peter and said, "Great to have you here. The more the merrier. Oh, yes, the more the merrier. WHAT A LIFE!" And he meant it. Peter could see it in

Santa's eyes, hear it in his voice; work and pleasure were one and the same. He was a lucky man. Clapping his hands, he ran off, only to come to an abrupt stop again.

"WAIT!" he roared, his round face etched with grave concern.

Everyone froze and the whole big room fell silent.

"Where're my *snacks* for the ride!?"

Throwing his arms up in exasperation, Harry stepped forward. "Every year, every year, the same thing, Santa. You worry too much."

"Well, I can't help it," he said like a little boy, hurt by the comment. "I get excited."

Harry stuck his fingers into his mouth, whistled loudly, and out came another snappy-looking elf, Kid Twist, pulling a small sled filled with cooked turkeys, some piping-hot pies, big red apples . . .

Santa took one look and was pleased. "My favorites. Thank you. I'm ready now," he said, relieved.

"Could you imagine if he didn't have a fast metabolism?" Harry said to Peter confidentially.

"Have a good ride, dear!" Mrs. Claus said, kissing him on his cheek.

"Always do. GOD, I LOVE THIS JOB!" he screamed, and for the last time, he charged out of the room. Kid Twist ran after him with the really long Christmas list trailing behind him. As Peter watched all this, his smile suddenly waned and he covered his face with his hands. Mrs. Claus noticed.

"Peter . . . ?" said Mrs. Claus. "What is it, dear?"

He paused, then replied softly, "I miss my wife."

"I know you do. But you have a family here now," she said gently.

"It's what I wanted to do with her."

"I know."

"Oh God . . . ," cried Peter, and Mrs. Claus draped her arm around his shoulder and he rested his head against her warmth.

## TEN

Cold. Barren. Lucy looked up and saw through the tears in her eyes the Manhattan skyline in the far distance, and if that imposing sight once made her heart leap with all its vitality and life, with all its irrepressible desire to keep growing and expanding, it was now a cruel reminder of what *wasn't* and where she stood. She was next to a priest in Potter's Field, and the biting wind whipped and slashed through the thousands of gravestones, tying an invisible thread all around the lost and forgotten souls who died penniless. It was nature's way of connecting them, telling us, however cruelly, that something, someone, far greater *had not* forgotten.

Lucy stood still and silent. Her thoughts were only with her husband, wondering how such a good, caring, and loving man could end up here. My God, Lucy thought. How did this happen?

The priest closed his Bible and dropped his head in prayer. Lucy walked slowly to Peter's gravestone, placed a small flower on top of it, then broke down and sobbed. The priest gently put his arm around her and braced her from falling to her knees. He mumbled words of comfort, telling her that in time, her pain would ease, but his words fell on deaf ears. For Lucy, time had no meaning. She was now living in the century of tears.

The sun had been down for hours when Lucy climbed the stairs to her fifth-floor walk-up. As she reached the second-story landing, a door cracked open and Mrs. Hardwick stuck her head out.

"I heard what happened. I'm sorry," she said.

Lucy paused, muttered, "Thank you," then resumed climbing the stairs.

"You going to be okay?"

Lucy stopped, surprised by her concern. She turned and faced her. "I think so."

An awkward moment ensued as Lucy waited, even hoped, for another kind word, and she didn't even care if it came from the nasty old Hardwick. She simply needed to hear a sympathetic voice. But instead, this is what she heard:

"Did he leave you with enough money for next month's rent?"

Lucy's eyes flared with hate.

"Is that what this is? Is that all that you care about? MONEY!? I just buried my husband!"

"Quit your yammering. I was just asking...," Hardwick snarled.

"You're not a person! You can't be! A person needs a heart! What kind of monster are you!?" Lucy screamed in anger and complete frustration, nearly compelling her to do something she wasn't brought up to do, like punch the old hag in the nose. To avoid this, Lucy charged up the stairs, but then she stopped. She wasn't quite finished putting that old shrew back in her place, so she turned back around and ran down the stairs and pointed her shaking finger right into Hardwick's face.

"You'll have your lousy rent money the day after tomorrow. Now go to the devil!"

Furious, Lucy ran back up the stairs, determined never to speak to that woman again. They both slammed their doors shut and the entire tenement shuddered with outrage.

Later that evening, the animals were all quiet and respectful as they kept a watchful eye on Lucy sitting at the table stacking her loose change, and counting just enough for rent and some food. She rose from the table, fed Rodger-the-Podger, put down a small bowl of milk for Montclair-Sinclair-Éclair, fed the fish and the turtles, petted the marsupials, covered up the parrots, and walked over to the bed. She couldn't get into it. It was too soon. There were too many memories. She whipped the covers off, threw them on the ground, lay down on the floor, and stared at the ceiling. She pulled at her snowflake pendant hanging around her neck, kissed it softly, then rolled over, put her head on top of her folded hands and tried to fall asleep.

## ELEVEN

If Santa were flying overhead, he would have thought the city streets had been covered with a pulsing, thick black cloth, but for the thousands of people walking under their dark umbrellas, it was just another day of having to endure the rains that had been falling for three straight weeks during this cool month of April. Walking anonymously within the crowd, Lucy furtively placed the palm of her hand over her raincoat and touched her stomach, not out of nervousness or concern for the well-being of her child, but as a simple reminder that Peter, through the life of the baby growing inside her, was still with her.

She absentmindedly stomped through a series of puddles and walked down the factory-lined Manhattan streets, where she passed an organ grinder twirling the lever on his box for his top-hatted monkey dancing in the rain. Lucy shook her head at the begging animal, turned down another corner, then stopped in front of a large factory. She reached into her pocket and pulled out the morning *Herald Tribune,* and before the rain made the ink run, she quickly checked the address and name listed in the ad against the sign above the factory door, which read: "The Siegle Watch Company." She jammed the paper back into her pocket, and then with all her energy pulled open the thick metal door and entered.

She sat nervously in a wooden chair facing the chain-smoking supervisor sitting behind his beat-up desk, and watched with disgust as he slowly withdrew the cigarette from his thin lips and blew a long, sinister stream of smoke. He repeated this action twice more before he snubbed the butt out in his filthy ashtray and finally asked, "You single?"

"Widowed," Lucy replied in a barely audible voice.

"What's that, honey?" he said, showing her his yellow teeth.

"I'm widowed. My husband passed away a few months ago," she said a little louder.

His fingers flicked at the edges of her application as he eyed Lucy for a full minute, then said, "The company *likes* single girls. You know the score. Married women want to settle down, have kids. They get themselves pregnant and then they hightail it outta here. Isn't that right, sister?"

"I'll do a good job," she said, returning his stare.

The supervisor leered. "Sure you will." He let his

eyes roam over her hair, her face, her eyes, hoping he would catch some sign, some inappropriate opening from Lucy—but that was never going to happen. Instead, all he saw was her cold, defiant stare.

He lit another cigarette, spit a speck of tobacco off his tongue, waited for it to land on the floor, then said, "You'll sweep and mop the floors around the workers and dump all the trash in the big bins. Any pieces and parts you find, you put 'em back on the tables."

"Thank you," she said, standing. "May I start now?"

"Sure, sister, whenever you want."

He reached across the desk, looked her straight in the eye, and shook her hand; but he didn't let go. Lucy pulled away, took a step backward, then spun around and walked out of the room. Smiling, the supervisor sauntered to the door, leaned out of the door frame, and watched her walk down the long pale green hallway until she disappeared around a corner.

Feeling sick, Lucy ran into the small, cramped "employees' room," leaned over a filthy wash sink, and ran some water over her hands and face. Once dry, she grabbed the blue smock hanging off a hook, put it on, then picked up a mop and pail.

## TWELVE

Peter and Kid Twist, each carrying a pail in their hands (a little one for Kid Twist and even that was difficult for him to manage), trudged across the frozen tundra and entered a massive cherry wood barn lit by white candles.

"How are you guys this morning?" Peter asked. And there they were, the "Magnificent and Faithful Eight"— Dancer, Dasher, Prancer, Vixen, Donner, Blitzen, Cupid, and Comet—all rising from their beds of golden straw inside their mahogany stalls draped with bright green garlands, speckled with red berries. Last to rise was their new friend Rudolph, with the illuminating red nose— number nine.

"So, did you all have a good sleep?" Peter asked again, patiently waiting for the reindeer to grunt and snort in response.

When they did, Peter laughed. "Okay, okay, I know

you're hungry," he said, as he opened their stalls. "What do you want for breakfast? Alfalfa or oats?"

The reindeer grunted and snorted some more.

"Come on . . . you all know better now . . . ," Peter replied. But Rudolph snorted again and Peter turned to him and said, "No ice cream for breakfast." They all grunted with disappointment and Peter and Kid Twist chuckled.

"So alfalfa it is, because I'll tell you what, guys . . . if I fed you what you really wanted to eat, you'd never get off the rooftops. I'm just looking out for your best interests," said Peter as he walked away, leaving Kid Twist behind, who was busy amusing himself making little funny faces to the reindeer.

"Hey, Twist," Peter called, shaking his head at the distracted elf. The Kid quickly grabbed his pail, and with a one, two, three—heave ho, ho, ho—lifted it off the ground and with great difficulty stumbled and tripped all the way to the other end of the barn, where Peter was now throwing logs into the stone fireplace. Twist dropped the little pail down with a thud and proudly helped Peter by throwing some big twigs into the fire. But then he took off running again to catch up with Peter, who had already walked away and was now on the other side of the barn, stirring the alfalfa with fresh cream scraped off the top of an opened milk canister. Twist stood on his toes, looked into the drum, ran his tongue slowly over his lips, then with a gleam in his eyes, looked at Peter. "Go ahead, Twist," he said with a smile, prompting Twist to happily poke his forefinger in and scoop up a dripping dab of cream, which he slowly licked clean.

## THIRTEEN

It was well past nine at night and the factory was empty except for a few other women sweeping and mopping up the floors. The air was hot, musty, and still, and Lucy was sweating. With great difficulty, she lifted an over-flowing garbage can, dumping it into a larger bin. As she put the can down, she suddenly doubled over in pain from a strong contraction. She grabbed her belly, looked down, and was horrified to see a small puddle of water on the floor. . . .

"Oh, my God . . . ," she gasped. She took a breath, wiped the hair from her face, looked up, and saw the supervisor staring at her. He had an evil look in his eye and with his crooked forefinger, he motioned for her to come to him. She returned his stare, picked up another garbage can, and dumped the whole thing—garbage can and all—inside the bin. She took a breath, then whipped off her dirty smock, revealing for the first time her very pregnant state. She threw it to the ground. Then she marched right up to him—and smacked him hard across the face.

He touched his cheek in shock. The women were startled. They couldn't believe anyone would have the courage and strength to do what she had done. One by one, all the women dropped their brooms and mops, kicked their pails and dustbins with their shoes, and started clapping, out of sync at first, then in unison, until their cheers reached a deafening crescendo and the walls of the factory seemed to tremble.

Lucy grabbed her coat, looked at all the women, gave them a thumbs-up, then quickly exited the factory.

The supervisor glared at the women, who abruptly stopped clapping. Their jobs were more important than their pride, so they grabbed their mops and pails, put their heads down, and started cleaning up again.

✳

The large surgical room was all white, except for the linoleum floors, which had turned a sickly yellow from age and one too many waxings; aside from a large clock ticking away like a tired metronome in need of winding and a framed picture of President Franklin Delano Roosevelt, the walls were bare. Already lying down on a sheeted metal gurney, Lucy shuddered while the doctors covered in their white gowns and masks snapped on their thick yellow rubber gloves and silently checked their instruments. No one said a word and Lucy was scared. None of this felt right. Why isn't anyone talking to me? she wondered. Why am I in a room so severe . . . ? And the smells, the horrible reeking medicinal smells . . . there's death in here, not life . . . I don't understand. . . . She slowly rolled her head over and saw through her cloudy eyes a nun carrying a thick rubber tube in her hands and Lucy shivered. I'm having a baby, she wanted to scream. It's supposed to be beautiful, wonderful, not like this! Alarmed by the hissing sound of gas, she quickly rolled her head in the opposite direction, then she looked straight up and saw a nun hovering over her with a dull, black mask in her hand.

"Don't worry, child. You'll be fine," said the nun.

Lucy wanted to scream, I MISS MY HUSBAND! but the gas mask came down over her face and she faded into sleep.

Two hours later, Lucy kicked and turned, finally waking up in a cavernous recovery ward. She was groggy. A wet rag was across her forehead; her whole body hurt. She lifted just her head and saw in the shadows hundreds of perfectly made, white-sheeted beds jutting out from both sides of the barren walls. Trying to regain her senses, she rubbed her face and saw a lone shaft of yellow light coming through a large window in the middle of the room and she now realized she was the only patient there.

"I want to see my baby," she cried. "I want to make

sure my baby's okay. . . . I need to know, please. . . . Is it a boy or a girl? Why isn't my baby with me!?" and her screams for some attention were suddenly met by a set of squeaky wheels making their way along the hard tiled floor. Lucy quickly propped herself up and saw a nun emerging through the semidarkness pushing a little bassinet, passing through the light now, coming closer, until Lucy saw the nun's face—hard and pasty, her eyes cold and impatient—and Lucy was certain the nun's devotion to her calling was based on something other than compassion. The nun stopped, knocking the bassinet against Lucy's bed, and Lucy shuddered. The nun leaned over, then mechanically picked the swaddled baby up and handed the little child to Lucy, who lovingly cradled the little girl.

"She's a little small, being born early and all, but we think she'll make it," the nun coldly explained as she crossed her arms across her chest.

"She's beautiful," Lucy said, letting her eyes wander slowly all over the baby's sweet face.

"We need her name," the nun said sharply.

"Ellie. Ellie Thompson," said Lucy without looking up. The nun started to write the name down and then stopped.

"Ellie or *Eleanor?*"

Lucy looked up and said evenly, "Just Ellie."

"That's a fine Christian name," said the nun in a curt, sarcastic tone.

Lucy continued to coo to her child.

"Do you have a place to live?"

"Yes."

"Because if you don't, the church can take care of her. Help her."

"We'll be fine."

"We know you're alone . . . and these are difficult times. Even more difficult for a single woman."

Lucy bristled. The nun's assumption that she was a mother out of wedlock went straight through Lucy's heart and she stared at the nun, gritted her teeth, and said, "Don't you dare. The child's *father* was my *husband*. I'm a widow."

But the nun remained aloof. "We'll give her a home. She would be in God's hands, in the *palm* of God's hand."

"She's *my* baby and *my* hands are just fine," Lucy said, staring hard at the nun.

"I'm sure," she said with a wave of her hand. "But *when* you come back, the church doors will be open for *her*." And she walked off and Lucy was thankful to be left alone. Thankful for little Ellie—Peter's daughter, our daughter—and she held their child tight.

# FOURTEEN

Little Ellie giggled and smiled comfortably inside the makeshift bassinet made from the bottom dresser drawer in Lucy's apartment. She was healthy and happy, despite eating mostly fruit for the past three months. Vegetables were scarce and, more often than not, too expensive for Lucy's pocketbook, which was getting lighter each day. Lucy peeled half a banana and scraped at the fruit with a spoon, feeding Ellie the mushy paste, which she gobbled up with relish; then she cried and kicked her legs because her throat was parched and dry. Lucy wanted to feed her the milk from her breast, but with her own lack of nutrition, she had none to give.

Lucy walked to the icebox and pulled out a small bottle of milk, prompting Montclair-Sinclair-Éclair to immediately slide across Lucy's leg, arch its back, and meow in hunger. Lucy looked down, saw the cat's empty bowl, but poured the last few drops of milk into Ellie's bottle. Montclair screeched in anger, then raced to Rodger-the-Podger sleeping peacefully in the corner, and out of frustration and because she was a cat, scratched his head with her paw. Rodger-the-Podger jumped up and snarled. Montclair took another swipe and that was it. The two were instantly embroiled in a terrible fight and all the other pets woke up from their hunger-induced sleep, quickly chose sides, and started chirping and squawking for their hopeful winner while Montclair and Rodger belted each other like heavyweight champs with their claws and paws.

Furious, Lucy jumped into the middle of the fray, and after a lot of swinging and kicking, managed to separate them, and the cat and the dog skulked into the corner, where they curled up together in a heap and fell immediately to sleep. But Lucy wasn't finished. She stood in the middle of the room and yelled at all the other pets for encouraging their friends, explaining to Montclair and Rodger (who had no choice but to wake up) how they had to work together to get through this difficult time. Then she stopped, realizing she was talking to a bunch of parrots, marsupials, fish, cats, and dogs, and who knew what else her husband had picked up off the streets. She grabbed her head in frustration and thought, I must be going crazy. She sat down at the table, rested her head on her hand, and tried to make sense of her situation. She loved them all, no doubt, took good care of them, but she also had to feed her daughter and, sadly, she reached a decision. It meant she would have to lose one more tangible memory of Peter, and she looked at the pets and they all stared back with melancholy eyes. Needing to rest, Lucy picked little Ellie out of the dresser drawer and carried her over to her bed, where they instantly fell into a deep sleep together.

The next morning, Lucy gently nudged little Ellie's sleepy head off her chest, slid out of the bed, and quietly dressed. Then, tiptoeing across the room, she carefully picked up the birdcage still covered with a sheet from the night before and furtively carried it out of the apartment and into the hallway, where she placed it down in front of another apartment, knocked on the door, then tiptoed quickly back into her apartment, closing the door quietly behind her. She then picked up the aquarium, the marsupials, the turtles, and the hamsters, everyone except Rodger-the-Dodger and Montclair-Sinclair-Éclair, and carried them all out of her apartment, depositing each of them in front of her various neighbors' doors.

After breakfasting on a piece of toast and some jam, Lucy bundled Ellie up warm and tight, tagged a leash to both the cat and the dog, and with her arms now filled, walked out of the apartment and down the creaking stairs, making sure she stepped gently and quietly to avoid the wretched old Hardwick. She made it safely all the way to the front door, but when she stepped outside, she almost dropped everything as the harsh morning sun temporarily blinded her.

Squinting, she looked to her right and saw a little neighborhood boy sitting on his stoop playing a solitary game of jacks. She paused for a brief second, deciding within that time that he would be the perfect candidate to raise a dog and cat. Just as she was about to make the offer, a voice called out to her.

"Picture, ma'am? Only ten cents."

Lucy turned and saw a neatly dressed young man in his early twenties with a Bellows camera attached to a tripod slung over his back.

"I'm sorry, I can't," she said quickly, fully knowing she didn't have a spare dime to her name, so she turned back to the little boy—

"That's a beautiful little girl you have there," the photographer declared.

"Thank you," Lucy replied, when it dawned on her. She faced the photographer and said, "I'll trade you the dog for a picture?"

He tapped his fingers against his lips as he mulled over the offer and said, "I'll take the cat. They eat less."

Lucy accepted, and the photographer quickly set up the camera on the sidewalk. Lucy walked down the stairs, stood in front of the tenement, pulled out her snowflake pendant so it was visible over her coat, held Ellie up, posed, and POP!—the light bulb exploded. The young photographer whipped the plate out of the camera, jammed it into his bag, slung his tripod and camera over his back, and politely took the cat from Lucy.

"Thank you, ma'am. My wife will like her," he said

kindly. "And don't worry, I'll bring the picture by later."
Then he walked away.

Smiling, Lucy turned to the little boy still sitting on
the stoop and finally handed him the dog.

"He's for you."

The kid grabbed Rodger-the-Dodger and patted his
head. "Thank you, ma'am. I'll take good care of him."

"You look like you will," she said knowingly. She
walked away, saw a small piece of coal in the street and
picked it up, shoving it deep into her coat pocket as she
marched down the block.

Tired from walking, Lucy climbed the stairs of the
local library and walked into the reading room, where
she passed a matronly librarian who quietly and pleasantly said, "Morning, Lucy." Then she touched little
Ellie's cheek saying, "And how's my dear little girl?"

Lucy answered, "Growing beautiful as ever," and
their daily ritual wasn't completed until the librarian
handed Lucy the morning newspaper, which Lucy carried to a long, well-lit reading table, joining countless
others who had nowhere else to go. Lucy nodded her
hellos, then sat down, plopped little Ellie onto her lap,
unfurled the paper, and read it in a whispered voice,
from cover to cover—even the ads—to her little girl.
After that, she read countless children's books, but in the
back of her mind, Lucy knew these words could not
replace food for long.

PART TWO

CHRISTMAS, 1934

## FIFTEEN

The apartment was virtually bare. Anything that could have been pawned had been. Lucy sat on the bed with Ellie, feeding her some mashed dates while reading an old, beat-up-looking children's book she had borrowed from the library, when suddenly there was a knock on the door. Lucy got up, opened the door, and standing with her hands on her hips was Mrs. Hardwick.

"I want last month's rent," she snarled impatiently.

"I'll get it to you tomorrow," Lucy said, tired and defeated.

"How? Tomorrow's Christmas Eve. Where're you going to get me my money on Christmas Eve!?" screamed Hardwick.

Lucy closed the door in her face.

The next morning, Ellie woke up in her dresser drawer cold and crying from hunger. Lucy jumped out of bed, slipped on her robe, then, just as she did the night before, rifled through the cupboards, looking for something, anything, to feed her daughter, even though she already knew there was nothing left. Nevertheless, she was compelled by her raging mind to frantically open and close the cupboards, over and over, refusing to accept the unseemly absence of food; and it was only after she had completed the process of searching and ultimately seeing nothing again and again, that her mind released its grip on her and let reality emerge. She could not feed her child, and knowing this, Lucy collapsed to the floor crying. Then anger replaced her tears and she pounded her thighs with her fists until they were bruised and puffy. It wasn't until she heard Ellie cry that she realized that neither her tears nor her anger were going to put any food into her child's mouth.

What am I going to do? What would Peter do? Then it hit her—a wonderful thought. She saw it simply and clearly and she felt alive and excited as she quickly dressed little Ellie, bundled her up with every piece of clothing that fit, grabbed her own coat and scarf, tied the scarf tight over her head and around her neck, and with Ellie in her arms, ran out of the apartment.

It was brutally cold outside, and the wind made it difficult for her to run. Within minutes, Lucy, with Ellie propped up next to her, was sitting on a park bench tearing at a tiny bit of stale bread that she had traded for her piece of coal. I know this is going to work, Lucy said to herself. She threw some bread crumbs at the pigeons circling before her, and sure enough, one of the pigeons got close and Lucy carefully, quietly, pulled a pillowcase out from her coat and flung it over the bird. But it got away. That's okay, she thought, dismissing her first failure. It's only a matter of practice. I'll get the rhythm, just like that old man in front of the Plaza Hotel. She checked the small stale piece of bread she had in her hand and carefully broke off a tiny crumb and started all over, and within seconds, another pigeon came close. She whipped the sack down and missed once more. She tried again and again, over and over, missing by inches, each and every time, until she had but one tiny crumb left in her hand. She closed her eyes tight, fought off her weariness, then with a quick flick of her wrist, threw the crumb and waited for a pigeon to get within her range. It did, and she threw the sack over its head, but it darted away.

*

Old men in tattered coats and faded fedoras shuffled slowly forward until they reached the front of the line, where they gratefully accepted the day-old loaves of bread given to them by the uniformed Salvation Army workers. Lucy, with Ellie pressed tight against her chest, walked among those men. And with each step forward, Lucy grew weaker, but her eyes never strayed from the sight of the bread and it gave her the strength to continue. Finally, when it was her turn, she reached up, and with a shaking hand snatched the stale loaf of bread.

Without bothering to take a step away from the line, she tore off a piece, gummed it to make it soft, then placed it inside Ellie's mouth for her to eat. No one, not the Salvation Army workers or the hundreds of men standing behind her, desperate themselves for food, dared to ask her to move out of the way. After Ellie swallowed, Lucy dropped her head, leaned into the hard cold wind, and walked away.

As she turned the corner, Lucy jammed a small piece of bread into her own mouth, then braced herself for the long walk home. The streets were empty and dark. There wasn't a single light on in any of the office buildings, and even though it was Christmas Eve night, all the holiday lights hanging from store windows were turned off. Indeed, she was enveloped in complete and total blackness and her loneliness was so complete she felt nothing else existed in the world, save her and and her little baby. She headed down yet another long block, then abruptly stopped, lifting her head just in time to see the final farewell seconds of a shooting star fall from the sky. "Peter," she said softly. She looked back down at her child and started to cry.

Back inside her apartment, Lucy dressed Ellie in her finest outfit, slipped her into some sweaters, then swaddled her in some warm blankets and placed her gently inside a small wicker basket. She checked to make sure she was snug and comfortable, and Ellie's smile assured her that she was. Lucy walked to the table, sat down, and carefully composed a note. Once done, and after rereading it, she then picked up two pictures: one of Peter, smiling in front of their home back in Iowa, and the other, taken just the other day, of Lucy holding little Ellie outside their apartment. She tucked the photos inside the basket, folded the note, and placed it under the top blanket. Finally, she took off her crystal snowflake pendant, draped it over her child's head, carefully tucking it under little Ellie's sweater. Once that was done, she leaned down and kissed Ellie on the forehead, put on her coat and scarf, picked up the basket, opened the door, and walked out, not bothering to close it behind her. She walked slowly down the stairs, making her way past the second-story landing, when suddenly, Mrs. Hardwick's door flew open.

"Where do you think you're going?" Mrs. Hardwick cackled harshly.

"Out," Lucy said dully.

"You owe me rent. I got bills to pay!"

Lucy kept walking.

"I'm going to throw all your crap out, rent the place to somebody respectable."

"Do what you want."

"I'm not letting you back in. You'll see. I'm calling the coppers!"

"Call them," said Lucy without any concern whatsoever.

"GET OUT! GET OUT!" Hardwick shouted, and Lucy ran down the rest of the stairs not because she was ordered, but because she didn't want Ellie to hear Hardwick's screams. She gently pushed the front door open with her foot and walked out of the apartment building for good.

The bitter cold wind sliced right through her and Lucy felt naked. She stopped, put the basket down, took off her scarf, and used it as another blanket for Ellie, hoping one more layer would protect her from the relentless chill. She picked up the basket and walked wearily through the empty streets, saying softly to Ellie the whole way, "I love you, I love you . . . ," until she came upon a gated fortress-like building made of dark, church-block granite. She looked up and stared at the top of the wrought-iron gate where the metal was twisted and snarled into the words: "St. Vincent's Orphanage." And Lucy paused, too tired to continue. She pushed against the heavy, creaking gate and walked along the windswept path where a few brown leaves, cracked and forgotten from the season past, scampered and swirled along the frozen ground in search of some warmth.

She climbed the stairs and approached the doors of the orphanage. Still holding the basket, Lucy looked over and saw the lighted windows decorated with wreaths, and she could hear the nuns inside singing Christmas carols to the sounds of a blaring organ. She placed the basket down in front of the thick wooden door, got down onto her knees, draped her arms and body over the basket, and covered her daughter with hugs, then kissed her forehead until her tears fell on Ellie's cheeks. Lucy quickly brushed them away, and before she stood, she reached into her coat pocket, pulled out the rattle she had bought last Christmas Eve, and placed it in Ellie's hand, who immediately shook it and smiled. Lucy rose, walked to the door, knocked loudly a couple of times, then without looking back, walked slowly down the stairs, along the path, closing the iron gate behind her—leaving behind the orphanage, and with it, her child, forever. As she walked down the block, she could still hear the voices singing, "Oh, come, all ye faithful."

Now alone in her basket, little Ellie looked up at the starry night, smiled, and shook her rattle, while the nuns sang their carols, but the cold winter wind started to howl louder and she began to shiver.

Lucy continued to walk through the empty streets, but what was the point? She stopped on the corner, stared at the street lamp, first green then red, green, red, and for the life of her, Lucy could not justify another step forward, let alone decide which direction to turn. Instead she stood, not thinking, not moving a muscle; she was in all respects dead, until a hansom cab rode by, with no passengers in the back, but perched on the driver's seat was Peter—"My God! It's my Peter," then she cried out, "Peter, Peter!" and the driver turned around and it wasn't. She put her head down, stepped into the street, and started walking again—down a series of deserted streets all the way to the Bowery, where she passed grown men, drunk, barely alive, but asleep on the sidewalks, and she shuddered wondering where *their mothers were.* She prayed that her baby would be fine, now that she was in the "hands of the Church," in "God's hands," which gave her hope that she would see her daughter again, when she was older, of course, and wiser, and then she would explain it all to her. I have to keep walking, I have to continue, she thought. Otherwise my little girl will never know the truth— never know where she came from, never know how much I loved her, and Lucy knew there was no greater pain for a child than not knowing that. Nothing could compare, not even the pain she was suffering now. As heartbroken as she was, Lucy walked down another block until she came upon a two-story tenement with a partially illuminated sign over the door that read: "Women Only."

Behind the battered reception desk, a thin, wrinkled lady quickly hid her flask inside her housecoat and asked what Lucy wanted.

"A room."

"You mean a bed," the woman replied.

Lucy barely nodded.

"Fifteen cents a night, or a buck a week," said the lady, bored with the routine.

Lucy slid three pennies across the desk and the lady looked at them, then eyed Lucy. "That's it?"

"Yes," she said sadly.

With her eyes never leaving Lucy's face, the wrinkled lady pulled the flask out from her dress, slowly unscrewed the top, drank, then said, "Ahhh, it's Christmas Eve . . ."

But she raised her crooked finger and warned, "Just this one time . . ."

She scooped up the pennies and handed a filthy little pillow to Lucy, which she clutched tight against her chest. The wrinkled lady pointed to a frayed curtain on the other side of the lobby and Lucy walked toward it, pushed it aside, and her eyes immediately teared up from the hot, musty stench emanating from the room.

Once inside, she stood before hundreds of metal beds with floppy mattresses and stared into the hollowed eyes of the abused, the tubercular, the homeless, and the just plain unlucky women who couldn't make it in the city. She wanted to run, but she knew she couldn't. There was still some hope and Lucy clung to that thought as she walked slowly into the room, passing these indigent women, convincing herself with each and every footstep that she was different, much different. She was Lucy Thompson, born to Jedidiah and Ellen Johnson of Iowa, the mother of Ellie, the widowed wife of a good and proud man. Look at me, her soul screamed, I SAID LOOK AT ME!, *my head is still held high!* By the time she found an empty bed at the back of the room, she realized none of that mattered, because she was now, just like everyone else in the room, alone. She lay down on her bed, fully clothed and . . . began to sob.

## SIXTEEN

Harry stood in the middle of the big room and looked at the clock, its candy cane hands tick-tocking until they hit exactly 11:55 P.M., and he screamed: "Five minutes, everyone!" and it was madness all over again.

Using all their might, Kid Twist and Nutter dragged two large red sacks as they raced to Santa standing in the middle of the room. He grabbed the sacks from their little hands, heaved both over his shoulder, and spun around only to see Harry standing in his way.

"Here's a bag of coal," said Harry, handing Santa a small bag.

Santa grimaced. "Can't we come up with something different for the bad little ones? It's messy."

"Tradition," Harry said. "I'd give wilted cauliflower myself, but did anyone ask me? No. So take the coal."

Reluctantly, Santa obeyed, mumbling, "Who was the crazy knucklehead who thought of that one?"

Harry said, "You did."

"Forget I asked," said Santa and he spun around, faced his family of regulars and elves, and smiled with happiness.

"Okay, let's do it," he yelled. "It's Christmas Eve, my favorite day!" All the elves and people jumped up and down, wildly clapping and cheering, "Go, go, GO!"

Teeming with pride and overwhelmed with love, Santa's face turned bright red: "Great job this year! Thank you all. Couldn't have done it without you." And Harry polished his nails against his vest, thinking, That's for sure . . .

"And let me tell you," Santa continued, "I have a great feeling about this one! You betcha. A great feeling!"

Everyone cheered some more.

"So, I'll see you all in the morning! And if I'm not too tired, I'll make you all my special breakfast of pancakes with a side of roast beef, some sausages, some big hunks of bacon, potatoes, yams, and huckleberry pies!"

More cheers.

"Merry Christmas! Merry Christmas!" Santa sang, and everyone went crazy, jumping up and down again, throwing confetti into the air, popping little streamers, banging pots and pans with metal spoons, and blowing kazoos. Santa grabbed Mrs. Claus, planted a big kiss on her lips. She cupped his round face in her warm hands and said sweetly, "I'll miss you tonight, so come back soon, safe and sound."

"Always do, sweetheart," and he leaned in for another

kiss, but they were interrupted when Harry slapped him on the back.

"All right, all right! My brain is starting to freeze with all the mush. Let's go, boss, we got a job to finish. The reindeer are ready and waiting."

Santa grabbed his sacks, waved good-bye one last time, and ran out of the room.

Charging into the stable, he saw Peter wiping down the polished sleigh, checking the garlands and red velvet ropes that tethered the reindeer together, tugging at the leather reins, making sure they were taut (but not too taut), and finally giving each and every reindeer their traditional and final snack—a gingerbread cookie. They had wanted chocolate fudge sundaes, but traditions were hard to break in the North Pole, so they settled (as if they had a choice) once again for the cookies.

"Ready?" Santa asked.

"All set, Santa," said Peter, whipping around with a smile.

Santa threw the sacks into the sled, then hugged Peter.

"All these years, Peter, and I still get excited," Santa confessed.

"That's why everyone loves you."

"But after all these years, I still have never gotten used to the takeoffs."

"You'll be fine," Peter said reassuringly.

"And Rudolph is ready?"

"He's all set. Prepped and eager."

Santa smiled. "His maiden voyage . . ." He scooted

over to Rudy, patted down his nose, and said, "Don't worry, kid, you'll be fine."

Rudy snorted and thanked Santa for giving him the chance, promising him that the beacon on his nose would work fine on this foggy night and that he wouldn't let him and the other eight down, and on and on until all the other reindeer snorted, saying, "All right already, you'll be back before you know it, kid."

Embarrassed, Rudy clammed up fast, put his head down, thinking he had made a fool of himself, but he hadn't. He was young, that's all, and Santa was charmed by his enthusiasm, so everyone was all square.

Santa climbed into the sled, took hold of the reins, barked a gentle, "Ho," and the massive barn doors magically opened, revealing the perfect white tundra under a gorgeous starlit evening speckled with shooting stars flying in every direction. With a whoosh, the cold air flooded the barn and Peter tightened his scarf around his neck.

Santa nudged the reindeer forward with a gentle pat of the reins and they trotted out of the barn, their feet stepping softly on the icy snow, slowly making their way to the precipice of a hill, where they stopped, because just then a tall red sign popped magically out of the snow that read: "STOP!"

Santa expertly wrapped the reins tighter around his hands, leaned forward, peered over the reindeer, and looked down a massive ski jump that was at least a mile long. He took a long, deep breath . . . wiped his brow, looked up just in time to see the sign flip green with the words: "HAVE FUN!" flashing, and Santa smiled.

"Okay, Rudolph. Let's bring them some happiness!" Rudolph's nose turned bright red and WHOOSH!—off they went. The reindeer galloped like crazy down the hill, faster, faster, until their ears were pinned back and their feet hardly touched the ice, and WHAM, faster they went down the hill, and with one hand Santa grabbed his cap from flying off and with the other, he held on to the reins for dear life, screaming the whole time, as loud as he could, "Ho! Ho! Ho!" As they came near the edge, Santa let out a final, glorious "Ho!" and—liftoff! The reindeer and the sled flew up and out, disappearing into the heavens.

Peter could still hear Santa's "Ho's" drift through the starry night as he closed the barn doors behind him.

That night in Paris, France, a little girl lay in bed awake with anticipation. She looked out her bedroom window, saw Santa and his sleigh high in the sky racing toward the Eiffel Tower, and when he passed over it, the entire structure lit up. She smiled, happily whipped the shades shut, and hid under the covers. She was a believer and *she knew* he was going to come to her home and in the morning, she was going to find more treats than she had ever imagined, hoped, or even asked for.

Moments later in London, England, Santa's sleigh zipped past Buckingham Palace, and the palace bells began to rattle and clang! The next morning, all the children throughout England would still hear those bells ringing in their hearts as they opened their magnificent gifts wrapped perfectly in green and red paper.

Seconds later, in New York City, a poor little brother and sister with dirty faces sat looking at the sky through a small cutout window inside their crudely made tin shack nestled amongst hundreds of others in the middle of Central Park. When they saw Santa and his sleigh racing with blinding speed toward the Statue of Liberty, they pointed, and just as he flew over it, Lady Liberty's torch ignited in a burst of flames. They smiled because they were believers too. In just a few more hours, they were going to find under their tiny little Christmas tree made of broken branches and fallen acorns scavenged from the park, little cakes and tasty apples for them and their family to eat.

Santa's sleigh landed with a thud on a Manhattan rooftop. He grabbed a sack, jumped out, ran over to the tiny chimney, and magically squeezed himself through. He landed at the bottom of the fireplace and looked around. Instead of seeing socks hanging from the fireplace, he saw a bunch of old tattered shoes. He quickly jammed them with presents, and as he pulled his sack toward the tree, he was startled by a noisy racket coming from the chimney. Curious, he dropped the bag, walked back to the fireplace to investigate, and was knocked down by Rudolph, who came falling, stumbling out of the chimney in a rush. They both scrambled back to their feet.

"What are you doing?" Santa said in a harsh whisper, fearful he might wake the children. With apologetic eyes, Rudolph looked at him, sniffed the air, turned around, and eyed the cookies and milk the children had left for Santa.

"Oh, no you don't!" said Santa.

But Rudy licked his chops.

"They're for me!" Santa protested.

It was a standoff. They stared at each other, then at the cookies, then back at each other. Who was going to make the first move? Santa bolted for the cookies, but Rudolph, slipping and sliding on the wood floor, beat him to it, and with one big swoop of his tongue, gobbled up all the sweets.

Santa was furious. "GET UPSTAIRS. RIGHT NOW! I'M MAD AT YOU!" he said as loudly as he possibly could. Rudy put his head down, sheepishly grunted something about how he had a sweet tooth and it was all entirely out of his control, but he was working on it as best he could—that it wasn't an issue of character, but one of behavior, and in time and with a little work, he felt he could change—until Santa felt profoundly guilty and even terrible for yelling at him and tears welled in his eyes as he draped his arm around Rudy and said, "I understand, I really do," because he did.

"But it's hard," sniffed Rudy, "I try and try, but . . ."

"Oh, Rudy . . . ," Santa said, with his heart breaking. "I know you're trying. Me too, but there are times when even I can't help myself and I just have to eat a couple of pies and cakes and then I feel bad . . . but we can't be so hard on ourselves or each other."

"You're right, you're right . . ."

"We just have to practice a little moderation, that's all . . ."

"That's what Donner has been saying," said Rudolph, "but look, Peter has to keep expanding my harness . . ."

"Oh, so what . . . You're young and you're growing. Look, I'll make a deal with you," Santa said, as he reached inside his coat and pulled out six cream puffs he had secretly stashed away, handing three of them to Rudy, which were gratefully accepted. As they ate, Santa continued. "Next time you get that feeling, Rudy, and you want to sneak out of the barn and raid the cookie jar, call me and I'll join you. We shouldn't be alone in this. Deal?"

"You're the best, Santa."

"And you're going to be fine, Rudy . . ."

They washed down their cream puffs by sharing the glass of milk, and then with a couple of loving pats on Rudy's rump, Santa said, "I'll meet you upstairs."

Rudy wiped the tears from his eyes, thanked Santa again for being so understanding, sauntered back to the fireplace, then magically shot up the chimney to rejoin the others.

Feeling proud and energized by their little heart-to-heart with his new leader, Santa quickly dropped a few presents under the tree, then flew up the chimney, where he too popped back onto the roof, all covered in soot.

The reindeer took one look at him, rolled their eyes, and after grunting three times, they snorted hard and loud, blowing all the soot off Santa's face and suit, leaving him clean once again. Laughing and still wiggling from their warm gusts of air, Santa jumped back into the sled and off they went.

## SEVENTEEN

It was dark and quiet at St. Vincent's Orphanage. The Christmas caroling was over and all the nuns were tucked inside their warm beds. Even the shadows had gone to sleep since the moonlight was now obscured by the heavy snow falling on Ellie's tender cheeks as she lay unattended outside in her basket. The snow fell harder and Ellie wailed in frustration. Her arms and legs flailed in every direction, knocking the picture of her father loose, which a great gust of wind caught, carrying it, along with her plaintive wails, up into the sky where Santa was flying by. He heard the cries, but he barely paid attention, figuring it was just another disappointed little boy or girl who snuck out of bed in the middle of the night and found a bag of coal under the tree instead of the presents they thought they deserved.

The cries continued, and even though Santa sailed

through the sky faster and farther away, the cries not only seemed to follow Santa, they seemed to be getting *louder.* How could that be? he thought, and why won't they stop? He was steering his faithful nine toward his next destination, when suddenly his heart and his soul were pierced by a long, forlorn call for help *and that did it.* No child should be left to cry that long and hard. He pulled the reins sharply to his left and the reindeer quickly veered off-course, banking around and down to the city, getting closer and closer to the cries, until Santa and his sleigh screeched to a stop on the walkway in front of St. Vincent's Orphanage.

Santa quickly jumped out and saw little Ellie crying and thrashing in her bassinet. Smiling, he slowly leaned down and gently wiped the snow off her face, and she immediately stopped crying. He looked around and saw no one, and a look of concern and confusion crossed his cheerful face. He picked her up and bouncing lightly on his feet, held her tight against his warm red suit. Out of the corner of his eye, he noticed the note sticking out from under her blankets. Ever so carefully, he leaned back down, pulled it out and unfolded it, reading it silently at first and then aloud:

> *My heart is shattered, my soul, bent and broken, for I could not give this most deserving and beautiful child a chance in life. I leave her to you, to keep her safe and comforted in the palm of God's hand. Her name is Ellie.*

*Please love her as much as I do. God forgive
me.*

*—Lucy*

Santa jammed the note into his pocket and paced. He
didn't know what to do. He looked up at the orphanage
door, then back at the baby girl still in his arms. . . . Still
unsure, he paced some more, then he heard little Ellie
shake her rattle and laugh, and a smile crossed his face,
and in one fluid move, Santa placed her back into the
bassinet, covered her with the blankets, then picked up
the whole thing, raced to the sled, put her in the backseat, jumped in, whipped at the reins, and with his precious cargo, off they went, zipping through the heavens,
heading *not* to another house, but straight *back* to the
North Pole.

The seals saw him first and they realized he was coming in fast. Standing on their hind legs, they clapped and
barked, then waddled away, revealing Santa's magical
house once again. The sled landed with a bunch of skids
and bumps, and before it came to a screeching stop in
front of the red front door, Santa had already hopped
into the backseat, checked on little Ellie, who was still
smiling and shaking her rattle, grabbed the basket, then
jumped out of the sled, and raced toward the house.

Inside, the elves and the regulars sat around relaxing,
drinking cider, smoking cigars. It was, after all, their one
and only night off. When the door burst open, they
jumped to their feet at the sight of Santa standing there!

Something bad must have happened, they all thought, because Santa never, ever came home early.

"Where's Mrs. Claus?" he barked.

Frightened, Kid Twist stepped forward and asked in his little voice, "Santa . . . ? What are you doing here? You're supposed to be delivering all the gifts."

"Never mind that, Twist. Where's my wife!?" he yelled. "And put out those cigars. I have a little baby with me!"

Everyone quickly snubbed them out. Twist nervously swallowed his in one gulp.

"Now, where is she?" he shouted.

Twist waited for the cigar to land in his belly before saying: "In the kitchen, roasting chestnuts on the fire."

Santa's black boots left prints on the floor as he stormed out of the big room and toward the kitchen.

Kid Twist spun around to Nutter, but he spun so fast he couldn't stop spinning, so Nutter reached out and grabbed him, saving Twist from screwing himself deep into the floor.

"What do we do?" he said.

Still cross-eyed, Twist mumbled a "thanks," then his eyes straightened out and bulged. "HURRY, GET HARRY!"

This time, Nutter jumped up, spun his legs like an eggbeater, hit the ground running, and was gone.

Santa kicked open the kitchen door, startling Charlotte, who dropped the teacup from her hand.

"What happened . . . ?" she asked, deeply concerned.

Santa froze, said nothing. He looked down at little

Ellie, who was cooing softly, sweetly. Charlotte took a small step forward and saw a tear streaming down Santa's cheek.

Santa looked up and softly said, "I have something for you . . . I mean for us."

"What . . . what is it, dear?"

Santa pulled back the scarf covering little Ellie's head, then held the smiling child up for Charlotte to see.

"Honey, this year we received a gift," he said gently.

Mrs. Claus walked closer, touched the baby softly on her red cheeks, and her heart fluttered as she took a deep breath.

"She's beautiful . . . ," said Mrs. Claus, with awe in her eyes and love in her heart.

"And special," confirmed Santa.

"Who is she?" she asked, now stroking the baby girl's head.

"Her name's Ellie. Her mother couldn't care for her. She was all alone, crying in the cold, the snow was on her face . . . and she was so helpless . . ." And Santa's chin started to quiver and he began to cry. "She was so sweet . . . she's just a baby . . . I couldn't bear it, I couldn't leave her . . ."

"It's okay, it's okay," said Mrs. Claus, gently stroking his arms and shoulders. Santa cried so hard with joy, his knees began to buckle. Charlotte tried to take the little girl from his arms, but he wouldn't let go.

"All these years, Charlotte," he said, stumbling

through his tears, "all these hundreds of years, we've been taking care of children. We've done well, we've done real well with them, Charlotte, but in my heart, I've always . . . I always dreamed . . . that we would have one of our very own."

"Oh, Santa . . . ," said Mrs. Claus, knowing that she too had the same silent dream.

"We can give her a good life, Charlotte . . ."

"I know . . ."

"She'll never be cold again . . ."

"Never . . ."

"Our little baby. She can be . . ."

"Ours . . . ," Mrs. Claus said, completing the thought.

"Yes, our own little Ellie Claus," he said, smiling through his tears.

"I love you so much . . . ," she said, and she wrapped her arms around them both.

Suddenly, Harry bashed through the door and froze. He surveyed the situation, rubbed his eyes, then blurted out, "Have I gone snow blind or is that a baby in your arms!?"

Santa spun around beaming. "Charlotte and I have just adopted a little girl. Meet little Ellie," he said, and he presented the baby to Harry, who took a quick look at the child and thought, Yeah, that's real sweet, then turned to Santa and said, "Boss, I think that's great, I really do, but *tonight* you decided to do this? Your timing, know what I'm saying?" And he tapped his watch impatiently and his voice grew to almost a shout. "Because, Santa, last I checked, IT'S CHRISTMAS EVE!"

"Isn't she beautiful?" Santa replied as he cooed over Ellie, completely disregarding Harry's appeal.

Mrs. Claus gently took the baby from Santa's arms and carried her over to the rocking chair in front of the warm kitchen fire, sat down, and plopped little Ellie onto her lap, rocking her back and forth.

Santa stood over them making crazy faces at the little girl. Then he leaned in close.

"Can you say, Ho, ho, ho?" Santa asked Ellie, who smiled and laughed at him.

"Will you look at that! She's beautiful and she's got a sense of humor too!" Santa said proudly.

Harry grabbed his hair and started to pull.

"Santa, you're the boss, so you can pelt me with a thousand snowballs for saying this, but I think it's time you get back on your sleigh!"

Santa protested by bouncing up and down like a little kid. "But I have a baby to take care of."

"And you still have a *hundred fifty million kids* to visit in seventy-two countries. So if I were you, I'd shake a leg there, BIG GUY!"

"He's right, dear," added Mrs. Claus.

"Thank you, Mrs."

Charlotte gave Santa one of those "You better go now" looks.

"All right, in a second," said Santa as he leaned back down and tickled little Ellie's chin.

"Harry, we're going to need a few things," said Mrs. Claus.

"Okey-dokey," replied Harry impatiently. As he opened the kitchen door, he saw Kid Twist and Nutter jump away from the keyhole, then run under his legs and into the kitchen.

"Whatta you guys . . . ?"

"Congratulations!" roared Kid Twist, but Nutter knocked Twist in the arm and complained, "I wanted to say it first."

"Thank you," said Mrs. Claus. "But can you get us some diapers and bottles, please?" Kid Twist and Nutter nodded, then charged for the door.

"Wait!" yelled Santa. The two elves skidded to a stop. "First, we have to hug her a lot. Everybody has to give her lots of hugs!" he demanded.

"Okay, dear," said Mrs. Claus patiently.

"And tell her she's pretty all the time," he said excitedly, as if reading off a list.

"Okay, honey. You'd better get going now."

"And tickle her, that's important, and just like this." And he demonstrated the correct technique for everyone to note, making little Ellie laugh again. "See?" said Santa.

Mrs. Claus put up her hand to calm Santa down, then turned back to Nutter and Twist.

"Twist, don't forget some pillows, please, the goose down ones."

And off they went again.

"Wait!" shouted Santa. SCREEEECH! Twist and Nutter stopped so fast, they carved a three-foot-long trench into the floor.

"And we have to comb her hair all the time and say sweet things in her ear, like, 'Who's the prettiest, smartest little girl in the whole North Pole?' Stuff like that," he said, beaming.

"Honey, you have to leave right now," Mrs. Claus pressed.

"I'm going . . . ," Santa said without moving a muscle. "But we have to tell her we love her all the time."

Harry was about to explode. "Santa, they got the Depression going on down there. They need you more than ever. It could be a BLOODBATH!"

"Harry, really . . . ," said Mrs. Claus, thinking Harry was getting a touch too dramatic.

"I'm sorry, Mrs., but it's like trying to move an iceberg, know what I mean?" whined Harry.

"All right, I'm leaving," said Santa, no longer having a choice, because Twist and Nutter were now leaning like Atlas into Santa's back, pushing him toward the door. Just as they gave him the final heave, Santa twisted his neck around managing to add: "And don't forget to make her feel secure, protected, confident. That's very important!" BAM!

Harry slammed the door shut behind him, took a deep breath, pulled in his stomach, snapped his suspenders, then addressed the elves like a general preparing his troops for battle. Twist and Nutter eagerly stood at attention waiting to hear the command.

"Okay, now listen carefully!" said Harry, and the elves leaned in closer. Harry took a deep breath, then said simply, "We got some work to do. Let's skeedaddle."

Wow, thought Twist and Nutter, What a plan. Comprehensive and big! All the angles are covered. Boy, Harry's definitely got everything under control, and they dutifully skipped and hopped behind Harry as he marched out of the kitchen.

Outside, Peter walked out of the barn just in time to see Santa jump back into his sleigh, snap at the reins, and streak back to earth. If that left Peter dumbfounded, then the sight of Kid Twist hastily painting the name "Ellie" under all the other names on the mailbox certainly left him flabbergasted, and his jaw moved like a nervous puppet as he asked Kid Twist what the heck was going on.

"Don't you know?" proclaimed the elf. "Santa and Mrs. Claus adopted a baby!"

Shocked, Peter took off running, slipped and slid on the icy snow all the way to the front door, barged in, and ran like a hungry schoolboy straight for the kitchen.

Peter whipped open the door, saw little Ellie crying in the arms of Mrs. Claus, and he froze.

Charlotte looked up and smiled. "Are you okay?" Mrs. Claus inquired. "Peter . . . ?" she said a little louder, and Peter snapped back into consciousness.

"Sure, I'm fine," he said, and he passed his hand across his face and came closer.

"She's beautiful," he said as he leaned down and gently stroked the baby's chin, not noticing the crystal snowflake pendant tucked inside her clothes. Ellie looked at him, stopped crying, and smiled.

"You seem to have a way with babies," said Charlotte gently.

"My wife and I, we wanted one," he replied softly.

"Her name is Ellie."

"Ellie . . . ," Peter whispered. "My wife loved that name." He paused, then smiled again at the little girl. "Well, nice to meet you, Miss Ellie. And what a looker you are. Those eyes . . . She looks like, just like . . ."

"An angel?" Mrs. Claus said.

And Peter kept staring at the baby but he agreed, "Just like an angel."

Harry charged into the big room and shouted, "Okay, everybody, back to work! Santa and Mrs. Claus have a new baby and her name is Ellie, Ellie Claus!"

Chaos! The room erupted in cheers. Harry continued, "We need diapers, *lots* of them, and bottles, and rattles, and things for her to chew on, little pajamas, and those new little slippers. You know, the ones with the pinwheels on the front, the ones Macy's stole from us, the ones that are selling like hotcakes down there. And we need baby clothes, soft stuff—all cotton, with lots of pink ribbons and frilly things. Make everything pink. Pink and maybe a little yellow."

The crowd jumped up and chanted, "Three cheers for Ellie! Hip hip hooray!"

"Now get to work, because we need those diapers now, and *fast*, know what I mean!?" shouted Harry.

Everyone downed their cider, smacked their lips dry, snubbed out their cigars, and raced back to their work stations. And as Harry watched them run around like dervishes, crashing into each other, and pretty much making a mess out of the room, a big smile crossed his face. He pulled a large cigar from his vest pocket, jammed it into his mouth, and lit it with style. He decided he was glad for the boss and the Mrs. That little Ellie, he thought, she's going to be good. Wish I had one myself . . . but hey, that's why I'm here, and he hitched up his pants and puffed away joyfully.

❊

Later that night, Santa's sled screeched to a stop on top of a rooftop. He jumped out of the sled, ran to the chimney without his sack, ran back to the sled, leaned into the back, pulled it out, ran back to the chimney, and instead of squeezing himself through, he dumped the gifts out of the sack and onto the roof, blew on his hands, rubbed them together, then grabbed a couple of presents and flung them down the pipe. The presents flew through the chimney, and out of the fireplace down below, only to land, magically and perfectly, under the expectant tree. Santa spun around and faced the reindeer, who all shook their heads and grunted in disapproval.

"I'm sorry," said Santa, embarrassed, his cheeks a little more red than usual. "But we're running out of time and I have to get back to see my little Ellie."

He chucked a few more gifts down the chimney and turned to Rudolph. "Okay, pal, let's get going."

Rudolph's nose lit up and WHAM!

The reindeer flew off the roof forgetting Santa, who remained on the roof, screaming, waving his red sack. "Hey! Wait for me!" he yelled, then he jammed his fingers into his mouth and whistled loudly, which finally got their attention. They circled back and Santa jumped in, saying, "Wait till I tell Harry what you just did."

PART THREE

CHRISTMAS, 1945

# EIGHTEEN

She wore eyeglasses now and her hair was shorter and pinned back; she was still attractive, but she was not the same. Eleven years had passed since Lucy had left little Ellie on the doorsteps of the orphanage, and the years of not knowing anything about her child had taken a toll on her psyche. She wasn't bitter or angry. She wasn't impatient or judgmental. She was worse: indifferent and still, choosing to be passive by allowing life to happen without her influence, quietly melding into a larger context and feeling pleased for not being noticed. She stopped being curious about the world or the people around her; she preferred to be alone and found comfort consumed by her own questions and thoughts of her daughter. Was she big and strong now? Was she happy with the family she was living with? Was her hair long and braided?

When Lucy dreamt of little Ellie, it wasn't about the momentous occasions they would have experienced together, like the first ballet recital or the first spelling bee at school. No, Lucy dreamt of the small, ordinary moments that one takes for granted: seeing, in her mind's eye, the concentration all over little Ellie's face as she ate her first ice cream cone, watching Ellie fumble as she tried to comb her own hair, seeing herself smile as she waited patiently for Ellie to pick out that special hat before going on a walk, throwing Ellie up in the air just to see her mouth pop wide open with excitement, hugging her for no other reason than just to feel her warmth and softness, or just putting a bandage on her scraped knee and telling her that everything was going to be okay, because I'm here to protect you, my sweet little girl, to protect you with my life. Not being a witness to all this and more, broke Lucy's heart and she remained silent.

Lucy quietly turned off the light on her desk, locked the top drawer, grabbed her coat and scarf, and walked away from the stacks of compendiums and resource guides she used every day to help anyone find whatever information they needed, or track down any one of the millions of books housed in the main branch of the New York Public Library. In short, she was responsible for finding anything, and the irony of that was never too far from her thoughts. She passed the night janitor on her way out.

"See you tomorrow, Mrs. Thompson," he said with a respectful smile.

"Good night, Vinny."

Lucy walked through the main doors, down the steps, and disappeared into the crowded Manhattan streets.

It was a different time and place from when she had first arrived in the city. The Depression was over and the city bustled with energy, and with just four days to go before Christmas, the streets and sidewalks were packed with people getting their last-minute shopping done. Lucy put her head down, clutched her purse tight, and passed men in military uniforms, looking not for bargains but for pretty young ladies willing to take a chance on their name, rank, and serial number. She passed haberdashers and clothing stores advertising zoot suits for fifteen bucks, music stores selling "Benny Goodman Sheet Music" for a dime, and signs to "Buy War Bonds."

She turned off Fifth Avenue, headed west, and stopped in front of a small playground, where she leaned against the fence and watched the kids in school uniforms play, all eleven-year-olds, the same age Ellie was now. She scanned the crowd slowly, and intently looked into the children's eyes, wondering if she would recognize her daughter. She did not. Not today. She put her head down and walked away.

# NINETEEN

With her pigtails trailing behind her, Ellie raced through the big room, where, under the encouraging and watchful eye of Harry, the elves and the regulars were busily hammering and sawing, stitching and tying; they poured vats of pink, yellow, green, and blue goop into funny-shaped molds that were popped into the back of the ovens, only to emerge on the other side as airplanes, cars, pick-up sticks and jacks, dolls and bicycles, bats and balls, clothes and candy of every size and shape. As all the different presents came off the ramp, the elves and the regulars grabbed them with gloves (because they were still hot) and flung them high into the air, where they were caught by others who, after wrapping them, chucked them to another group of helpers who sat partially hidden behind five massive books—the books of lists (and they were so large, it took three elves to turn a single page). After these elves matched the names against the toys, they stuck little name tags on all the presents and flung them back into the air, where they landed (gently of course) on a massive pile, where even more elves and regulars shoveled them into Santa's two red sacks. What an operation! and Harry was proud. Everything is moving like clockwork, he thought.

Ellie ran behind him, grabbed hold of one of his suspenders, pulled back, and then let it go with a SNAP! Harry and she laughed, but when Ellie grabbed a little multicolored ball off one of the ramps (and it was still hot) Harry hollered: "Hey, Ellie belly, we need that one! It's for Mike-y in Toledo . . . Now what am I gonna do?" but Ellie kept running. He shook his head, pulled out a fat leather book from the back of his pants and checked a few items, then yelled out, "Okay, Twist, let's make a 'Slinky' for Mike-y in Toledo." He slammed the book shut and smiled, saying to himself, Boy, oh boy, I'm gonna make some company down there a whole snow mountain's worth of money once they see THAT! Pleased with himself, he looked over and saw Ellie leap over a few elves napping on the floor, then charge into her bedroom, slamming the door shut behind her.

She loved it here, living in the North Pole. She had hundreds of friends to play with, regulars and elves, and it never bothered her that most of her buddies were at least two, even three or four hundred years old, because everyone living here was young at heart. She ate well too, that's for sure. Her mom was the best cook ever.

Everything tasted sweet and hearty, the cookies and pies, even the roasts or the great salmon some of the elves would bring back after ice fishing all day long. Then again, she never ate anywhere else, so she really wasn't the best judge.

It wasn't as if there were a lot of families living nearby for her to compare meals with, but that didn't matter either, because she had all the family she needed right here—her mom and dad and even Peter, whom she really loved. In fact, she spent so much time with him, she even considered him to be part of the immediate family. If anyone needed to find her, they'd always look in the barn first, because every day after school (and after finishing most of her homework) she would help Peter tend to the reindeer and seals, and they would laugh and cry the whole afternoon away, as Peter transported her through time and place with all his wonderful stories about Iowa and New York.

School was even fun. She learned from the best teachers in the world because all of them taught from their own firsthand experiences. None of this, "Okay, class, let's turn to page fifty in our torn-up, outdated social studies books and read what *they* say about China. . . ." When Ellie learned about ancient history, the Roman and Greek empires, for instance, she was taught by people who were actually there at the time! Professor Plato was her favorite. Funny man, she thought. Funnier clothes. Or when she studied art, she was tutored by some of the greatest sculptors and artists who ever lived. Da Vinci and Van Gogh, just to drop a name or two, and they were the ones who taught her how to draw and make clay pots from mush. Uncle Leo was a little stern, but she really liked her Uncle Vinny a lot, even though he was always threatening to cut off his nose or lips or any limb for that matter, if she didn't perfectly capture the light when painting that same bouquet of yellow flowers over and over again.

Math and science? Please . . . She got to choose between Newton and Einstein. Absolutely, even Einstein. As Ellie heard it, a few years ago, Albert had this theory about traveling really fast from here to there and time being elastic and all, but he was hung up on a few details, and since *her dad already knew all about that,* Einstein showed up at the North Pole, carrying in his arms a bunch of chocolate cream pies and Bavarian cookies, and he and Santa spent three straight days eating sweets while Al quizzed him on all sorts of things. Al was so grateful for the help, he promised Santa he would pop on up from time to time and be the North Pole's visiting professor. Everyone liked him, even Harry, but Ellie especially. She considered him family too, because, well, why not, she figured. Everything he talked about was relative to everything else, so she just assumed that's what he meant and that's who he was—a relative, Uncle Al. Besides, he always walked around with his jacket pockets stuffed with cookies, handing them out to everyone he passed and Ellie just loved those treats. Uncle Newt, on the other hand, always had his pockets filled

with apples, and when teaching in class, he would drop
everything just to make a point.

But best of all were the toys. Harry is definitely a
genius, she thought, but if she hadn't thought it, Harry
would have told her anyway. Pretty interesting man,
considering he used to be a shoe repairman back in
Brooklyn. Who would have thought he was blessed with
all that creativity? But then again, here in the North
Pole, everyone in their own way blossomed and did the
best they could. At first Ellie didn't understand why,
until it dawned on her. It was simple: Everyone thought
about the children first—make them happy and the rest
would fall into place—that's why it was so much fun.
But let's face it: Ellie had a lot of fun because she was living in a house filled with toys.

There were trains and toy cars, blocks and games,
marbles and jacks, the old standards, of course, but Ellie
was really lucky, because she was the first to try all the
new toys, like that "Slinky" that Harry just invented, or
those new dolls he came up with, that he called Barbie
and Ken, which the elves complemented with all sorts
of fancy clothes. She even tried that funny new game
(which Harry wasn't going to put into production for a
while) where one stood on a mat with different colored
circles, spun a wheel, and according to where the spinner
stopped, one had to place a hand or leg on a circle until
everyone got all jumbled up and contorted and fell
down. Harry was going to call it "Twister" after Kid
Twist, which made Twist real happy and Nutter very

unhappy. Harry promised Nutter he would name a new game for him soon, and every day Nutter would tug at his knees and ask, "Where's my toy, Harry? Where's my toy?" until Harry almost lost his mind. So one night, in a manic, deranged state, Harry mixed up some white goop, slopped it into a big pot, threw in a couple of sacks of sugar, bottled the goop up, and the next thing everyone knew, all the elves were spreading this "Fluff and Nutter" over their gingerbread cakes. Nutter was finally happy and he was so pleased with how good it tasted, he brushed his teeth with it every night.

Harry invented all the new toys and, lately, he and Einstein (when he stopped by for a visit) talked a lot about some new games having to do with "chips" and "computers," but Ellie couldn't follow it. All she knew was that Professor Plato sure was against the idea. She caught just snippets of his argument, hearing him jabber away in a bunch of different languages about these "chips" and "little batteries" (another new invention), both being *passive* and kids should be *active,* blah, blah, blah, and Harry accused Plato of being "behind the times," which, considering how old he was, was probably right. But poor Uncle Plato sure was mad— threw a lot of dishes in the fireplace, even bit a table with his teeth and lifted it off the ground. She never saw anyone do *that* before. But it didn't make any difference, because Harry had the final word and he and Uncle Al already planned to mix up some new goop in the near future, probably in thirty or forty years, drop it into some special molds, and make them anyway.

All in all, what mattered most to Ellie were her parents, whom she loved, and she was grateful, without knowing why, for being their daughter. Certainly, Santa and her mom were kind to all the children in the world, but they were especially sweet to Ellie. Each and every night, after dinner, Santa and Ellie would play a crazy game called "Chasing Ellie to Bed." They would start at the farthest ends of the house, and on the count of one, two, three, Ellie would take off, running like crazy through the halls, down the tunnels, zipping through one room, then another, slamming all the doors behind her as she ran away from Santa, who was huffing and puffing, yelling the whole time at the top of his lungs, "I'm going to get you!" Ellie would squeal all the way to her room, where she would hide under the covers and wait for Santa to barge through the door and tickle her until she laughed so hard she couldn't take it anymore. She and Santa would collapse on the floor, tired and exhausted, and then her mom would come in with a whole armful of books, and the three of them would read aloud together until late into the night. Every night. Couldn't beat that.

Ellie burst out of her bedroom, ran in circles around the big shop for a little while, then leapfrogged over Beethoven and Mozart, who sat facing each other, oblivious to everyone else, as they banged away (on their little toy pianos) a dueling rendition of their latest combined effort, which they called "Concerto No. Four Million in G minor" but which Harry called "Snowdrifts Without Any Drums." Ellie then ran toward the kitchen, where—

Santa sat at the table, tapping his fingers, trying to decide which to eat first: the roast beef or the cooked goose . . . No . . . no . . . no . . . perhaps I should start with the baked ham, but look . . . , and he gasped. Is that Blitzen on that platter?! That would be horrid. We don't eat venison here. Oh, I see, silly me. . . . That's a roast pig and mmmmmm it looks good. With his eyes glued to the roast, he called to Charlotte, "Sweetheart, you better remind me to get my eyes checked." Charlotte, without looking over from the stove, replied sweetly, "Yes, dear," and Santa, pleased with her answer, resumed his musing: But maybe I should start with the pies—apple and blue-berry, oh, yes. . . . And he picked up his fork, stole a quick look at Charlotte, who was still busy over the stove basting a massive, golden turkey, and he decided, Now that's the ticket! I'm waiting for the turkey—when he looked up and saw Ellie bounce in.

"Hi, Mom, hi, Pop." She grabbed a candied apple off the countertop and stuck it in her mouth.

"Hey, where's my kiss?" asked Santa, beaming. Ellie ran over, planted a juicy one on his cheek, and he smiled, forgetting all about his meal for a second.

"Finish all your homework?" he asked.

"Almost."

"That's my girl," Santa said proudly, without realizing that *almost* was like *close enough,* which doesn't count for much. But what could he do? Ellie was perfect in his eyes.

She cruised by the counter, grabbed a bunch of cookies off the baking sheet, and jammed them into her pockets.

"Dinner will be ready any second," said Mrs. Claus, looking up.

"Ohhhh, Mom, I'm not hungry."

Santa raised his finger. "Ah, ah, ah!" he said sweetly. "No pouting, we have a rule about that."

"I know, see you later. Love you, Mom, love you, Dad." And with that, she ran out of the back door before Mrs. Claus had the chance to yell out, "You forgot your coat!"

"She'll be fine," said Santa, and he watched his lovely wife, who was all the more lovely in his eyes right now as she plopped the piping hot turkey in the middle of the table. "Sit, let's eat," he said excitedly as he picked up his fork and knife.

Charlotte took off her apron and sat down. "I think we're spoiling her."

"Charlotte, there's no such thing," he said, smiling as he began carving the turkey.

Ellie skipped into the barn and saw Peter tending to the reindeer. She gave a fake cough and he turned around and grinned.

"Hey, whattaya say, whattaya know!?" he asked.

"Whattaya know, whattaya say?!" said Ellie right back.

"I say it's feeding time," Peter replied, and Ellie laughed at their routine.

"Tooty fruity."

"And hunky dory."

"Let's do it, Mister Big," she said.

"All righty." And he grabbed a couple of pails and dropped them in front of the reindeer, who grunted with great pleasure.

Ellie and Peter sat on a couple of ice blocks.

"Well . . . ?" said Peter expectantly.

She reached into her pockets and pulled out the cookies.

"Aces!" He grabbed two from her hand and they both ate.

"Hey, Peter . . . ," Ellie finally said.

"Hey, Ellie . . ."

"Tell me about the world again," she said and Peter smiled.

"Ask your dad. He's been all over. New York, Paris, London, Greece . . . magnificent places. He's seen it all."

"I know, but he's always in such a rush when he visits."

Peter realized that she had a point and said, "I guess."

"Then tell me about New York. Come on, tell me again about the Plaza Hotel."

"I've already told you about that a thousand times."

"Come on," she urged, jumping up and grabbing his hands. "Tell me how you and your wife would sit in that little park, eat roasted chestnuts, and watch all the fancy people . . . kings and queens . . . arrive in their big cars and horse-drawn carriages . . ."

Peter thought about that, then said wistfully, "Oh, she loved that . . ."

"Tell me, Peter . . ."

"It was spectacular," he said. And Ellie sat back down. "Everybody in New York would come and watch." He paused. "And one day I was going to surprise her. Get all dolled up and take her there myself. March right up, arm in arm, just like those kings and queens. A team of valets behind us, bouquets of roses in their hands . . ."

"White ones with extra long stems . . . ," Ellie interrupted.

"Red ones. And we'd stay in the biggest suite, drink champagne, dance all night. We were going to do that."

"But you were going to look funny wearing one of those monkey suits . . . ," Ellie ribbed him.

"No, silly," he corrected. "Black tails, with leather shoes shined so bright, they'd light up the night."

"And what about her?"

"A long white gown, studded with pearls, white gloves, a cap with feathers . . . her face . . . God, she was the most beautiful of them all . . . a song come true . . . her eyes . . . just like yours . . ." Then he caught himself, turned to her, made a crazy face, then started to tickle her. "Hey, what are you doing? Huh . . . What do you think you're doing?"

Laughing, Ellie jumped away from him, screaming, "Nothing!"

Peter was on his feet before she knew it and he chased her around the barn. "I'm going to catch you and feed you to the seals . . . ," he said, laughing so hard he almost fell.

"NO!!!!!" she hollered with delight.

Standing unnoticed by the door was Mrs. Claus, who held her daughter's coat in her hand and smiled as she watched them run in and out of the stables.

## TWENTY

Tired, Lucy entered her apartment and took off her coat and hat. It was small and cozy, filled with books and pets. There were cats, parrots in cages, turtles and fish in glass bowls, even a little pooch of a dog whom she simply called "Come Here."

She opened the icebox, filled the cat bowls with milk, sat down, turned on the radio, flipped the dials, and stopped when she heard a breaking news report about the European Allied advances. She faced the corner of the room and stared at a very small Christmas tree, with nothing on it. Frustrated, she grabbed the tree, opened the front door, and dropped it outside her apartment door, slamming the door with a thud.

The fireplace was ablaze in the living room. Mrs. Claus sat knitting in a large armchair. Ellie, in her pajamas, was curled up on Santa's lap. Everyone was content and happy. He opened a book and started reading.

" 'Twas the night before Christmas, when all through the house . . . not a creature was stirring, not even a—"

"Dad, can't we read something else?" interrupted Ellie.

"But this is my favorite. It's a real page-turner."

"Mom . . ."

"She's right, dear," said Mrs. Claus. "Pick another, Ellie." Ellie crawled off his lap, scooted over to the shelves, and started searching for another book.

"I don't get it," Santa protested to Charlotte. "This book is full of suspense, and the hero . . . the hero of this book is the greatest guy of all time . . . just the greatest. . . ."

"I know, honey . . . ," said Mrs. Claus, having heard Santa say this at least a million times now. But she was patient with the man.

"I found it," Ellie shouted excitedly as she pulled a large book from the shelves.

"Here, Dad."

He looked at it, and his face got all screwed up. *"The History of Veterinary Medicine?"* he asked incredulously.

"That's a good one," said Mrs. Claus with a smile.

Santa looked at her like she was crazy, but he was patient with his wife—he loved her and she was such a great cook.

"Ellie, dear, before your dad begins, can you run to my room and get another ball of yarn for me?" she asked, without taking her eyes off the sweater that was quickly gaining a left arm.

"Sure, Mom." Ellie hopped out of the living room, ran up the stairs, cruised down the long hallway, and into her parents' bedroom.

She flipped on the gas lamps and looked around the room for the yarn, but she didn't see any on the dressers or the night tables—lots of recipe books all over, but no yarn. She walked to the closet and opened the door, looked up on the shelves—Nope, not there. She got down on her knees and saw lots of boxes on the floor, opened a couple—all empty. She slid the empty boxes out of the closet, reached in, opened a few more. There were some shoes, hats, but still no yarn; so she moved all those boxes out of the way and crawled even deeper into the closet. She pushed and slid more boxes out of her way, then saw—What is it? she thought. She disappeared for a moment, then came back out of the closet, pulling with her a wicker basket—the very same wicker basket her mother, Lucy, had placed her in eleven years ago.

Curious, she rooted around inside the basket, and pulled out the small quilted blanket that kept her warm that cold night. She pressed it against her face, smelled it; there was something familiar about it. She reached in and found the crystal snowflake pendant that her mother had placed around her neck when she was a baby. She stared at it, reached back into the basket, and pulled out a picture. Her eyes studied a woman, holding an infant, stand-ing in front of a tenement. Ellie stared at the little baby, touching the picture with her small fingers, then she brought the picture closer, closer, closer to her eyes, studying the faces more carefully, the baby girl, then back to that strange woman holding the baby, then back to the crystal pendant hanging around the woman's neck. She lifted the snowflake pendant in her hand, looked at it again, then compared it to the pendant hanging around the woman's neck in the picture. It was the same exact pendant she held in her hands and Ellie suddenly felt alone and cold. She dove back into the basket and pulled out a note, read it quickly, taking in key phrases, and the words began to jump at her: "I leave her to you . . ." "keep her safe and comforted . . ." "Her name is Ellie . . ." She gasped in shock. What began as an adventure had turned into confusion, which suddenly and unexpectedly became a startling nightmare. No. It can't be, little Ellie thought. There must be a reason, some explanation that I'm too young to understand. She looked at the baby in the picture . . . then she read her name again in the letter. *Her name.* Her eyes burned through the page. "Ellie" . . . "Ellie" . . . "ELLIE!" She got up and ran out of the room.

Ellie stood in the doorway of the living room, clutch-ing in her hands the note, the pendant, and the picture. Her eyes, motionless, stared at Santa and Mrs. Claus, trying to understand, trying not to cry.

Mrs. Claus looked up, smiled, innocent of Ellie's dis-covery. "Find some?" she asked.

Ellie did not answer. Instead, she continued to stare at her mother, No, NOT MY MOTHER, someone else. WHO?! she wanted to yell, but instead she bit her lip and stayed quiet.

"What's the matter, dear?" Mrs. Claus inquired.

Ellie held the picture up.

"Who is she?" she asked. And Santa's face turned a sickly yellow and he reached for his heart, but then caught himself, managing to remain still and calm. His eyes searched his daughter's face, struggling to find the right words.

"She's . . . well, we were . . . of course we were going to tell you . . . ," he stuttered.

Ellie's knees began to tremble, then buckle beneath her. Seeing this, Mrs. Claus rose quickly from her chair

"Come here, dear . . ."

"No," Ellie replied, her chin and lips now quivering. "Is she my mother?"

Charlotte and Santa exchanged a quick glance, then Charlotte turned and faced Ellie.

"Yes . . . ," Mrs. Claus said hesitantly. "We were going to tell you when you were older."

"I'm old enough!" Ellie said sharply, and both Santa and Mrs. Claus were more shocked by her tone than they were by the truth of the statement, causing them to pause with the realization of their mistake.

"I'm sorry, we should have . . . ," Mrs. Claus replied genuinely.

Then Ellie murmured softly, almost to herself. "I feel so lonely . . ."

"No, Ellie . . . don't," said Mrs. Claus.

"I do. I do!" she protested. "Didn't she want me?"

Santa stood, then spoke softly.

"Of course, sweetheart," said Santa, standing, wanting to walk to her, but fearing it might be too soon. "She was young, alone, she couldn't take care . . ."

"It was the Depression," Mrs. Claus blurted. "Your mother couldn't take care of *any baby* at the time. *Not just you.*"

Ellie began to cry.

"You were so tiny and perfect," said Santa. "It was cold, you needed a home. Oh God, Ellie, please understand . . ."

"She loved you, dear, I promise. And she did what she thought was best," said Mrs. Claus, wanting desperately for Ellie to stop crying.

But Ellie couldn't.

"Who's my father?" Ellie asked, swallowing hard.

Mrs. Claus took a breath and said softly, "We don't know."

"I want to see her. I want to see my mother." And even though she was struggling through her sobs, her determination was clear.

"We don't know where she lives. Honest," said Santa.

Santa found you outside an orphanage. St. Vincent's . . . ," added Mrs. Claus. "In New York. There was just the note and the photograph."

Then, silence. Santa and Mrs. Claus looked at each other, then looked at Ellie, hoping, praying to themselves that this was all going to end soon, that little Ellie would not only appreciate the situation and what they did—but also understand there was never any malice or harm intended, that it would all be right again, and all would return to—

"I'm going," Ellie blurted.

Santa yelled, "No, you can't!" the blood returning to his face.

"Yes, I can!" Ellie shot right back. "And I don't have to listen to you, *you're not my father!*"

This time, Santa did grab his heart, which was now breaking in anguish, and he muttered in shock, "Ellie . . ."

"Ellie, please . . . ," Mrs. Claus said, worried about Santa.

"No! You should have told me!" Ellie screamed. "Liars. You're both liars!" She ran out of the room, leaving Santa and Mrs. Claus alone and terrified, because, for the first time in their long lives, they now understood what it meant to hurt someone.

Bundled up with all the clothes she could manage to put on—shirts, sweaters, two coats, three scarves, a couple of hats—Ellie whipped open her bedroom window, leaned out, and crawled down the slope of the roof, slipping and sliding on the ice until she lost her grip. She tumbled off the roof, fell two stories down, but landed safely on a small snowdrift. Rolling over, she got to her feet and ran as fast as she could along the snow-packed tundra toward the barn. With a lunge, she reached for the door, opened it, then raced to Rudolph's stall, where she quickly grabbed his reins and pulled with all her might to get the young reindeer out of his stall. But Rudy grunted fiercely. He was confused, concerned. Something highly unusual was happening here.

"Come on, Rudolph, we're going . . . ," she said, digging her feet into the floor and pulling as hard as she could.

But Rudy grunted some more and and dug his own hooves into the ground.

"To New York," she said frantically.

He refused to budge and Ellie kept tugging.

"They have ice cream and hot fudge sundaes there," she said, and that did it. Rudolph's nose quickly turned red and he happily trotted out of his stall. She jumped on top of him, yelled in her lowest voice possible, "Ho," and the massive barn doors opened and they trotted out, heading for the precipice of the hill. Ellie, just like Santa, peered over the reindeer's head and gasped at the sight of the long, treacherous descent of the ski jump.

"Hey, where are you going!?"

Ellie spun around and was startled to see Peter running after her.

"None of your business," said Ellie and she kicked her feet into Rudy's ribs. The reindeer took another step forward, triggering the red "STOP!" sign to pop out of the ground. Ellie looked at the sign, and gritted her teeth impatiently.

"Wait! Wait! You can't take Rudolph!" shouted Peter.

"Why didn't you tell me I was adopted?" she yelled.

"What!?" Peter asked in shock.

"Why didn't you tell me?"

"Because it wasn't for me to do. They're your parents."

"Liar! You knew! I thought you were my friend. I hate you!" She whipped back around, her eyes glued to the stop sign, waiting for it to turn. "Turn already. TURN!" she demanded.

Out of breath, Peter was almost upon her. Just then, Ellie saw the sign change to "HAVE FUN!" and she gripped the reins tight around her hands.

"Don't go!" Peter begged. Ellie turned around, reached into her coat pocket, pulled out the crystal snowflake pendant, and threw it to the ground.

"Give it to Santa," she cried through her tears. "He can remember me with that!"

She faced forward, pulled the reins, screamed, "HO, HO, HO," and Rudolph took off and down they went. WHOOSH! Peter ran to the edge and looked down, but Ellie was too far away and disappearing fast. Then he heard little Ellie's voice fly back up the mountain screaming "Hooooooooooooooo!" and he looked up into the starry night and saw them streaking away.

Distraught, Peter dropped his head and ran his hands through his hair. Then he noticed the pendant laying on the ground. He leaned over, picked it up, and took a step back. "No . . . ," he whispered to himself.

"She's not in her room! Have you seen her?"

Peter looked up and saw Charlotte charging toward him as he stood frozen on the precipice.

"She took off with Rudolph," Peter replied softly, still in a daze.

"Oh, my God . . . We'd better get Santa," Charlotte said, and she spun around, started to run toward the barn, then noticed Peter wasn't following. She stopped, turned, and waved impatiently at him. "Come on!" she urged.

Peter lifted his head, looked at Charlotte, then whispered, "This pendant . . ."

"Yes, I know. What about it?" she asked impatiently.

"This pendant . . . ," Peter said again, holding it up in his fingers.

"Yes, Peter. I know," she said quickly. "Ellie was wearing it the day Santa found her. Now, please . . . Let's hurry. We need to get Santa!"

"Charlotte . . . this pendant . . . is the same pendant I bought for my wife the day I . . . the day I died."

Within a flash of a second Charlotte closed her eyes. Her shoulders sagged and her chest sunk inward. Her hands, which only moments ago were clenched tight with fear, now appeared soft and relaxed. Indeed, her whole body seemed to wind down and drain itself of life.

Then, just as quickly and almost unnoticed by Peter, the blood rushed once more through her and she was again tense and anxious to find her daughter. She turned and ran out of the barn.

Peter quickly followed.

## TWENTY-ONE

It was cold and the wind cut through Ellie as she flew high over New York City. She looked down and saw the city lights twinkling below. Having never been there before, she wasn't quite sure where to land, but as she flew a little closer, she saw what looked like a landing strip—a long narrow road bordered with lights—and she pulled at Rudolph's reins and guided him toward it.

Rudolph knew where he was heading and he knew this wasn't a good idea, but Ellie was the captain of this ship, and rules are rules. So he had no choice but to obey her, and as they rocketed through the sky getting closer and closer, Ellie now realized this was a colossal mistake—but it was too late! They were coming in fast and straight for Fifth Avenue! The streets were packed with honking cars and impatient shoppers running, yelling. Everyone and everything was moving at speeds quicker than even Einstein could have imagined, because with just two days to go to complete their Christmas shopping, it was in fact a race against time.

As Ellie flew closer, children everywhere stopped walking, pulled their hands away from their parents' tight grip, and pointed into the sky with a look of confusion on their faces. Wait a second, they thought, we already saw Macy's Thanksgiving Day Parade. They searched the sky for the strings keeping the reindeer afloat, but there weren't any. They looked again, this time expecting to see Bugs Bunny, or Mickey Mouse, but aside from Rudolph, the sky was empty. They fidgeted, waiting for the floats, or the high-stepping marching bands to come around the corner, but when that didn't happen, they knew, *they knew,* and their mouths dropped and they screamed through their smiles, "It's Santa's reindeer!" "Mom, Dad, Pop, Grandma, Grandpa, Uncle John, Auntie Kitty, look, LOOK. IT'S COMET OR BLITZEN, MAYBE IT'S DANCER OR PRANCER, ONE OF THEM IS IN THE SKY. BUT LOOK, ITS NOSE IS ALL LIT UP AND RED! AND HE'S COMING IN FOR A LANDING!" Which Rudy was, fast and furious, red nose blinking, whizzing over their heads, mere feet above the cars, and Ellie could see all the children pointing and she waved. Happily, they all waved back, wondering, who was that lucky little girl and who was this special reindeer whom they had never seen before?

The parents, of course, had their heads filled with more important issues, like, How am I ever going to finish my shopping, get home in time to clean the house, scrub the floors, cook dinner, wash the clothes, set up the Christmas tree, and drape it with tinsel and angel hair, when my high-strung child here is slowing me down with his crazy hallucinations of seeing some red-nosed reindeer supposedly flying through the streets of Manhattan?! Okay, that's it! Your father was right. It's military school for you next year! And ZOOM! Rudolph glided down, successfully avoiding all the cars, buses, and trucks, and landed flawlessly and safely in the middle of the avenue. The children applauded, but the parents couldn't care less and they quickly dragged their kids away, marching them as they kicked and screamed right into the next department store.

Startled by the tremendous roar and the sights of the city, Ellie was unsure what to do next, so she stayed on top of Rudolph and tried to adapt to the sensory overload. Suddenly, a cab came to a halting stop beside her and Ellie flinched. The cabbie, who had just been humming "I'm Dreaming of a White Christmas" to himself and was clearly in a good mood, leaned out of his window and barked, "Hey, girlie, that's some ride you got there. Think Santa would lend me one for the season? I could make a lot of money with that!"

Ellie turned nervously away.

"Come on, kid, talk to me. What's the score with the blinking red nose? He must be a new one. What's his name?" the cabbie asked excitedly.

Ellie blurted out, "Rudolph."

"Rudolph with the red nose . . . I like that," he said smiling as he got out of his car and approached her.

Ellie remembered hearing stories about cab drivers from Peter and decided it was wise to avoid him. She jumped off Rudy and quickly whispered in his ear, "You'd better go. I'll meet you at George's stable. Santa told me all about him. He'll have some sweets for you."

Rudolph grunted with glee, knowing sweets were in his future, and he wagged his tail. She patted his back and he took off like a rocket. Ellie nervously spun around, saw the cabbie coming closer, then eyed all the cars and trucks barreling straight at her as she raced for the sidewalk, dodging a hansom cab . . .

"Hey, come back here!" shouted the disappointed cabbie. "Hey . . . it's okay. *I'm a believer* . . ." But Ellie was long gone and the cabbie scratched his head, and got back into his cab. Then he froze, hearing in his head a song tune, a marvelous, catchy melody. He quickly opened the glove box, pulled out a crumpled piece of paper, grabbed the pencil resting on his ear, and starting writing feverishly, humming the whole time, as he jotted down: "Rudolph, the Red Nosed Reindeer . . . Had a Very Shiny Nose . . . And If You Ever Saw It, You Would Even Say It Glowed . . ." And before he knew it, he finished the song, took a deep breath, and said to himself, "Boy, I wonder if anyone would want to hear this?" He thought about it for a minute, then said, "Nah . . . Nobody would believe it," and he chucked the paper out of the window. As he slowly pulled away from the curb, he saw in the rearview mirror a little boy pick up the paper, read it, smile, and then jam it into his pocket. Suddenly, a woman's hand smacked the little boy on the back of his head and the cabbie heard her scream: "Johnny Marks! How many times have I told you not to pick up trash off the streets. What do you think you're going to find, GOLD?" The little boy walked meekly away and the cabbie shook his head and kept on driving.

Ellie ducked inside a doorway and tried to catch her breath. She crouched down against the door, brought her knees to her chest, and shivered.

❅

"Wow, Rudy, you're two days early," said George as he watched Rudolph casually saunter into his stable.

Rudolph grunted and George listened. "Ellie, huh. Oh, boy. Well, take a rest. Want a banana split?"

"Sure do," grunted Rudolph, and his nose turned bright red.

## TWENTY-TWO

Harry jumped out of his seat and screamed, "YOU CAN'T DO THAT!"

"I can and I will, Harry! There will be no Christmas until I get my little girl back! Now, sit down," ordered Santa as he paced furiously throughout the kitchen. Harry sat back down while Peter, Kid Twist, and Nutter nervously fidgeted in their chairs around the table. Mrs. Claus jumped up next.

"Santa, please," she implored.

But Santa wasn't listening.

"Somebody better get down there fast, and soon, because I can't bear the thought that my little Ellie is down there in New York City all alone and cold."

It was Peter's turn to stand. "I'll go," he said. Then he turned to Santa. "Why don't we both go? We can split up, save some time."

Harry kicked his chair back. "Whattaya talking about?! Santa can't go! Those are the rules. He can only go down there on Christmas, so just forget it, okay!?"

"Then I'll go myself," said Peter.

"You think you can just go down there?" Harry shouted. "No chance! Not on my watch, Buster!"

"Why not?" retorted Peter furiously.

"Because I said so. It's over." Harry flicked his hand in the air, then he turned to Santa and said, "We'll send the elves. They can fly around real fast and find her. No one will see them."

Nutter and Twist dove under the table.

"This is no time for tricks, Harry!" barked Santa. "Ellie's smart. Peter can reason with her."

"And I know the city," added Peter.

"But he's got no powers down there!" argued Harry. "He's a regular guy. He's got this thing with the animals, but so what? Please, Santa. It's too risky. He won't have enough time. And rules are rules!"

Peter pushed Harry aside. "Stop! What are you talking about?" he shouted.

Suddenly everyone averted their eyes and stared at the walls, and Twist's and Nutter's teeth started to chatter, then their whole bodies began to shake until they were twitching so fast, their bodies became indistinguishable.

Finally, Mrs. Claus said, "Santa, let's think about this for a minute," and Twist and Nutter became still again.

"No. My mind's made up," Santa said and he turned

to Peter. "I want you to go down there, make sure she's safe. If she finds her mother, fine. They can say hello, talk for a little bit, but then you bring her back."

"Good!" Peter exclaimed with relief.

"It's not good! It's bad!" shouted Harry. "There're consequences!"

"Quiet!" yelled Santa. Scared, Kid Twist and Nutter covered their heads with their hands, then held their breaths for the inevitable.

"Tell him, boss. Tell Peter about the rules, already, and let's get it over with," Harry implored.

Santa eyed Harry, then he looked at Peter. His eyes were cold and steely. No one had ever seen Santa like this before. He spoke in a hard but measured tone.

"Listen carefully, my friend. We have rules. Just like in Heaven. And sometimes when there's an emergency on earth, an angel is sent down. But if the angel doesn't get back in time . . . ," he began, and he let the thought sink in. "Same thing here. You have forty-eight hours, with or without her, to get back to our North Pole. That's midnight, Christmas Eve." He paused again, then said, "Because if you're not back by then . . . you will turn into a comet—a ball of flaming rock, flying alone through the galaxies for all eternity, never landing, never stopping, never finding a home again. That's the punishment. Do you understand?"

Harry looked up sheepishly and caught Peter's eye. "I told you when you first arrived. Remember? Shooting stars, good, comets . . . bad."

Peter spun back to Santa.

"I'd better get going."

"Just bring back our little girl," warned Santa.

With a heavy heart, Mrs. Claus rose from the table and embraced Peter, kissing him on his forehead.

"Be careful and hurry home," she pleaded.

Peter turned to Santa for any last-minute suggestions or instructions.

"Take Comet. He's the fastest." Peter ran out the door.

"Good luck, Peter!" shouted Harry, and Twist and Nutter put their hands together and prayed.

## TWENTY-THREE

Ellie darted out of the doorway onto the Manhattan streets, ran down the block, turned the corner, and saw Santa there, ringing a bell! She ran up to him and grabbed him by the coat, screaming, "Leave me alone!"

"Hey, kid, what's the rub?" Santa spun around. He looked terrible. His beard was all askew, his face wasn't round and cheery at all, and his eyes were thin and watery. Ellie was shocked—this couldn't be—

"Who are you?" she asked.

"Santi Claus, whattaya think?" he snapped back, wiping his nose with the back of his hand.

Confused, she took a step back, almost tripping on her feet, turned around and saw another Santa Claus, then another and another. There were "Santas" everywhere, tall, thin, fat, every size and shape imaginable, all standing next to iron pots, ringing their bells, bells, bells, and the sound of those incessant bells became deafening in her head and she covered her ears with her hands, screamed, and started running.

✳

George looked up and saw Peter riding Comet like a jockey coming in for the finish, cruising right through the doors of his stable, and landing with a skid in front of him. George simply and calmly sucked on his cigar long and hard, and by the time he pulled it out of his mouth, the entire cigar was, from end to end, entirely ash, and it wasn't until George blinked that the long ash fell to the ground with a POOF and George thought, Whoozawhatztaknow, I just hope he has my ten bucks; but instead he exclaimed: "Peter!"

"Good to see you, George," said Peter as if they had spoken just moments ago and not eleven long years before. Peter jumped off Comet. "I'd love to sit and chat, but I gotta go find Ellie." As he ran for the door, Peter said, "Hi, Rudolph!" and Rudy looked up from his basin filled with a banana split, licked his chops, and grunted, "Hello."

"Hey . . . ," George called out and Peter stopped, turned back around.

George jumped off his stool, ran to the back of the stable, and reemerged pulling an old horse, tethered to a hansom cab.

"Take Dorothy here. She'll help you get around."

"Thanks, pal," Peter said, and climbed on top of the perch, snapped the reins, and he and Dorothy cantered out.

Watching them go, George suddenly grabbed his head with both hands and squeezed until his eyes bulged. He then let his hands go and his eyes snapped back into their sockets and his mouth popped open and he yelled: "Hey! What about my ten bucks?!"

❋

As was her daily wont, Lucy sat alone on the bench and gazed at the wealthy people walking in and out of the Plaza Hotel. A cold wind blew and she shivered. She pulled her wool coat tight around her neck, fidgeted in her seat, but she couldn't get comfortable, nor could she concentrate on her memories, which as each day, month, and year passed were becoming increasingly difficult to conjure; so she got up and walked away, thinking she mustn't return again. It's foolish, she thought, because what I did can never be changed and the outcome will always be the same. Worse, it was the Christmas season again, joy to all and glad tidings for the world, and just hearing that phrase in her head, in all its nauseating cadence, made her sick. Christmas had become the season of grief. As she walked out of the park, stealing glances at all the parents happily holding hands with their children, she knew she would return tomorrow.

Remembering what Peter said, and hoping he was right, Ellie ran into the little park, thinking: *Everybody in New York comes here.* She slowed down, caught her breath, faced the Plaza Hotel, and saw all the fancy cars ferrying the elegant men and women back and forth.

Ellie reached into her pocket and pulled out the photo of her mother. She stared at her mother's eyes, because even though Ellie was young, she was smart enough to know the eyes never change. She quickly scanned the crowd, then slowly, methodically, walked in circles around the park, looking into the eyes of each and every woman she passed.

After circling at least a dozen times, Ellie sat down, tired and defeated, and so was Santa, who stood alone on the frozen tundra in the middle of the North Pole screaming into the wind for his daughter to come back home.

## TWENTY-FOUR

Peter prompted the old horse Dorothy to trot as fast as she could along the busy Manhattan streets, and perched all over the hansom cab and tagging along for the ride were a dozen or so chirping birds.

"We need to put our noses to the ground and figure out where she went!" Peter said, and Dorothy whinnied sharply back.

"I know you're not a dog," Peter said impatiently. "I'm *not* expecting you to *sniff* her out. I'm asking you to send the word to your friends because I need all the help I can get." But that little misunderstanding prompted Dorothy to carry on endlessly about *dogs,* because none of this dog business made any sense to her and even though she was old and weak, Dorothy still considered herself superior to the canine family.

"I'm sorry. Just forget I said anything," said Peter,

but Dorothy was still upset and insulted, even confused as to how dogs ever became known as man's best friend, and she snorted: "I'm tired of this, got it? But let me ask you . . . who's leading this search? Me! Right? Me! Not some mangy dog, but me, a horse!"

Peter tried again to assuage her feelings by offering her a carrot, but Dorothy was too smart for that and she stopped dead in her tracks in the middle of the street, demanding to know: "Was it a *dog* that carried man on its back out west to settle this great country? Was it a dog that pulled the covered wagons and the stage-coaches and the great tree trunks over hills and dales for you to build the great stalls and barns you live in? No! It was a horse, like me! A smart, loyal horse, not some overweight, drooling dog who one afternoon pranced around the snowy woods carrying, and let me add, *barely carrying,* a small barrel filled with whiskey under its neck, and the next thing you know, he's famous and everyone loves dogs. Makes me want to eat rotten apples. Why, I was hauling wheat by the bushels before I was six weeks old, not some little barrel of whiskey the size of my nose, so please . . . You can take their little wagging tails in search of approval and feed 'em a bone for all I care!" To emphasize her point, she whinnied long and hard with disdain.

Peter knew he had bigger issues to contend with, so he quickly agreed, "You know, you're so right, silly me." Dorothy, pleased with her ability to convert yet another foolish human, nodded, and started walking again; then she snorted some orders, whinnied out a few contingency plans, and all the birds fluttering around the cab got the message loud and clear and they quickly flew off in every direction in search of little Ellie.

"Good, thank you," said Peter, secretly smiling, knowing a dog would never have given up so quickly.

✳

The Plaza Hotel was empty, not a guest in sight, not even a doorman shuffling back and forth trying to keep warm on this cold night, and curled up fast asleep on a park bench across the street was Ellie. Suddenly, a policeman's hand reached down and jarred her awake. Surprised, Ellie scampered to her feet and tried to scuttle away, but the cop grabbed her.

"Hey, kid, what's the problem?"

"Let me go!" she shouted.

"Hey, take it slow. Where're your folks?" he asked with genuine concern.

"I don't know," she said truthfully.

The cop noticed her dirty face and all the sweaters, coats, scarves, and hats she wore, and he thought this was definitely unusual, probably even some sort of clue to a crime she might have committed, or maybe she was just a runaway. Either way, he decided he should bring her down to the station house.

"Maybe you oughtta come with me," he said, and he grabbed her hand again, but she quickly wiggled out of his clutch and ran away as fast as she could. Shocked, the cop jammed his whistle into his mouth and blew hard, but by the time the sound of the whistle traveled past his lips, Ellie was long gone, snaking her way through the dark streets of Manhattan, looking for a safe place to spend the night. Concentrating on the rhythm of her breath, she suddenly remembered her mom, no, Mrs. Claus, saying: *"Santa found you outside an orphanage, St. Vincent's . . . in New York."* She stopped and asked an old beggar where it was, and after a little negotiation and some haggling, he walked away with one of her scarves and she was now in possession of directions.

It took hours for her to make her way through the maze of downtown streets, but she did. Tired, she looked up at the large iron gate—old and rusted with a massive chain secured around it, locking it tight. With her mittens wrapped around the cold bars, she peered through the gate. The building was boarded up, abandoned, and she dropped her head, feeling exactly the same way. There was no one to talk to, no one to guide her. Snow began to fall and she walked away looking again for a safe, warm place to spend the night, knowing she would start her search for her mom again in the morning.

As Dorothy trotted slowly through the streets, her lips flapped nonstop about the unreliability and unaccountability of birds: "Always flying off without a moment's notice, never staying put in one place . . . you can't trust them—they're not like horses—give us a bag of feed to bury our noses in, a couple of apples, throw in a carrot or two, and we stay put—you better believe we do . . . we're loyal . . . And can a bird move a tree trunk for you? Pull a stagecoach! Anyone ever bet on a bird race?! Huh? . . . I don't think so . . . !"

Peter rolled his eyes, looked at his watch, then turned to the sparrows chirping like crazy as they defended themselves against Dorothy's accusations. He then glanced over to the squirrels and mice now sitting in the back, and Peter couldn't tell if they were shaking the snow off their heads, which was now falling fast and furious, or if they were just shaking their heads in fear, knowing they were going to be next on Dorothy's hit list. He hoped it was the former, because he was grateful for their help and he needed all the eyes he could get to help find Ellie.

"And another thing," whinnied Dorothy. "Why am I pulling a bunch of squirrels sitting back there like kings and queens?"

Oh, no. Peter cringed. Here she goes.

"What have they ever contributed aside from teaching us all bad manners? What, their mothers never taught them it was impolite to stuff their mouths with food?"

Insulted, the squirrels stood on their hind legs and shot back, "Well, you chew with your mouth open! And your big tongue wags all over the place, and we think that's disgusting!"

"What do you expect me to do, you rotten little runts, I don't have little, tiny hands to hold my food. I have hooves . . . great big, strong hooves, but you wouldn't know that, because you're all too busy jumping like monkeys from tree to tree, greedily stuffing your mouths with nuts! You call that a life?!"

Peter shook his head, rubbed his face, looked at his watch again, then saw all the people on the sidewalk, pointing and staring at him surrounded by the squawking animals. "Oh, boy," he muttered to himself, and just then a few birds, exhausted from completing their first reconnaissance mission, landed on his shoulder and Peter quickly asked for an update. The birds chirped wildly and Peter's grim face said it all: "All right, I don't see any kids either. . . ."

He snapped the reins, and Dorothy yelled out, "Take it easy, pal . . . I know a couple of dogs who could use that, but *not me,* brother. I'm a horse, old, maybe, even a little weary, but I'm still a horse and a lot more powerful than those mice grabbing a freebie back there! Do I look like I'm scared of them? Do I look like an elephant or something?" And off they went.

❋

Trudging through the snow, and feeling colder than she'd ever felt before (it was a "wet slushy cold" here in New York, not the "dry cold" like back home in the North Pole), Ellie saw an entrance to the subway and quickly headed down the stairs. She ducked under the turnstile, shook the snow off her hat and coat, and walked along the deserted platform. Suddenly, she heard a roar of unimaginable power rumbling toward her. She whipped around and saw the terrifying face of a train barreling through the tunnel. Its eyes, wide and bright, beamed with anger and its mouth was locked and clenched tight, and Ellie thought if she didn't hide right away, the train would certainly devour her. She ran to the end of the platform and saw standing, side by side, two broken vending machines, filled with stale sticks of gum, and between the two, there was just enough room for her to sneak in and hide, which she did. Wedging herself in, she sat with her back against the wall, pulled her coat up around her neck, pressed her knees against her chest, and covered her ears as the train thundered by. She cried herself to sleep.

## TWENTY-FIVE

"What's wrong with all of you?" Lucy said as she rubbed the morning sleep from her eyes, wondering why the animals were making such a racket. "What the heck is going on with all of you? Come Here," Lucy said to the dog, patting her knee with her hand, but "Come Here" wouldn't budge from the center of the room. Instead, he barked at the top of his lungs, and his bushy tail wagged back and forth so fast, it left the wood floor sparkling with a badly needed shine. The parrots squawked, the cat meowed, and little tidal waves appeared inside the fish bowls caused by the guppies blowing air bubbles out of their gills like they were auditioning for Esther Williams. They were beseeching her, saying something terribly important, but unfortunately, she couldn't understand them. Frustrated by all the noise, Lucy gave up, ran into her bedroom, and quickly dressed for work.

✳

Ellie opened her eyes and saw hundreds, if not thousands, of legs, some in pants and shoes, others in stockings and high heels, walking past her. She managed to slowly squeeze herself out from the two machines, stand, then stretch her arms and legs for just a second, before being instantly propelled down the platform by a series of pushes and shoves from the oncoming crowds.

The snow had stopped falling and the sun appeared briefly, but the sky was still milky and dense with winter clouds. Nevertheless, the fresh air felt good to little Ellie as she walked down the tenement-lined street looking for 314 E. 8th Street, which was the address that appeared in the picture of her mother that she held tightly in her hand. Eyeing all the front doors and counting down the numbers as she went, Ellie finally stopped in front of an old decrepit structure that she was certain was abandoned. The front door was splintered and mangled, hanging on with its life to its rusted hinges. The windows were shattered and all that remained inside the frames were tiny shards of glass sticking out like so many shark teeth. It was dark and evil-looking, and Ellie shuddered with the thought that her mother, or anyone else for that matter, could have lived here.

Ellie checked the picture against the address again, confirming she was at the right place. As she walked up the worn slate stoop covered with melting snow, she was startled by the sight of a nasty, older-looking lady, thin and weary like the stick of the shovel she held in her hand. It was Mrs. Hardwick.

"Excuse me, I'm looking for a woman named Lucy," said Ellie very politely.

"Whattaya, a cop?" spat Mrs. Hardwick, already looking for a fight, and since this kid was alive and breathing, why not her.

"I'm eleven years old," said Ellie innocently. Mrs. Hardwick eyed her and pulled out a small bottle of brandy from her tattered coat. She took a swig and Ellie waited patiently for her to put the bottle away, before she handed Hardwick the picture of her mother. Hardwick scanned it, then shoved it back into Ellie's hands.

"Yeah . . . I remember this one. A real deadbeat. Didn't pay her rent. Left a parrot in her apartment. I twisted its neck, cooked it up, and ate it. Yum." And her breath, visible in the cold air, swirled out of her mouth in a long, thin stream.

"You're not very nice," blurted Ellie, and before she could cover her mouth with embarrassment, Hardwick's face turned green and leathery.

"Listen, kid, I've been hearing that for years. Didn't bother me then, doesn't bother me now, so beat it if you don't like it!"

She took another swig of her brandy, jammed it back into her coat, then started shoveling the snow off the stairs, dumping the wet slop all over Ellie's boots.

Ellie kicked her feet free of the snow, saying, "She's my mother."

Hardwick stopped shoveling. She turned slowly around and stared at the little girl.

"You're the little baby in the picture . . . *You're Ellie?*" she said, a little surprised.

"Yes, ma'am," Ellie replied simply.

Hardwick paused, propped the shovel against the door, walked down the stairs with a small smile across her face. She approached the little girl, leaned down, then with her thumb and forefinger held Ellie's chin and stared into her eyes. She took a deep breath and then— shrieked: "So what do you want from me! You here to pay me the money she owes me . . . HUH?!"

Ellie had heard about heart attacks and now she thought she was having one. She jumped back and said, quivering, "No . . ."

But Hardwick wasn't finished.

"I'm all alone. Everyone's gone. Your mother, everyone, they all left me, bunch of louses! The bankers are coming any day now, take my building away. What about me? Where am I going to go? Huh? You ever think about that?"

Silence, except for the heavy wheezing coming out of Hardwick's chest. Finally, Ellie summoned the strength to look in her eyes and say: "I'm sorry. But do you know where my mother is?"

"Couldn't care less." And Hardwick whipped out her bottle and took another slug and marched back up the stairs.

Ellie watched her go, then she dropped her head and began to walk away.

Mrs. Hardwick turned around. "Hey, kid, wait!"

Ellie stopped, turned slowly, her eyes tired and sad.

"I'm sorry. Maybe it's the booze."

Ellie nodded as if she understood what she meant.

"Listen, I heard your mother got a job working with books. Always heard her reading, reading, reading to you when you were just a baby. With all those words she poured into your ears, you better be the next Shakespeare, that's all I have to say." She paused, then said softly: "Check the library."

"Which way?"

"North. The big one on Fifth Avenue. The one with the lions out front."

"Thank you."

"Maybe you'll find her," Mrs. Hardwick said genuinely.

"I hope so," said Ellie, walking away.

"Hey! If you need somewhere to go . . . I'll rent you a room. I'll give it to ya cheap. This town ain't a nice place for kids."

Ellie continued walking down the street, until a cold shiver overtook her and she froze. She saw Peter come around the corner in his hansom cab! For a brief second, they locked eyes, then she quickly spun on her heels and hightailed it as fast as she could in the other direction.

Peter couldn't believe his luck. "Ellie!" he shouted, then he frantically snapped the reins, and good ol'

Dorothy quickly maneuvered the hansom cab around
and she galloped down the street, blowing past Mrs.
Hardwick, who stared in wonder at all the commotion.

"Ellie . . . !" Peter screamed again, over the "clompty,
clompty" sounds of Dorothy's shoes pounding the pavement. But Ellie kept running.

The hansom cab careened around the corner on two
wheels—and all the animals slid and crashed against
each other as they piled up in a heap in the backseat. But
Dorothy kept going.

Ellie made it all the way to Fifth Avenue. She quickly
slowed down, caught her breath, and blended into the
crowd. But being so small, it was difficult for her to see
over all the people walking in front of her, so she hopped
like a pogo stick until she finally saw the two great lions
sitting on either side of the main entrance of the New
York Public Library. Excited, she took off running like
a bandit, and before she knew it, she was already taking
great leaps and bounds, hurdling over two, three steps
at a time, making it to the top of the staircase in a matter
of seconds. Out of breath, she leaned against the revolv-
ing doors, turned around, and quickly scanned the
streets. Good, he's gone, she thought until she saw Peter
pull around the corner. Frustrated, she grimaced, then
instantly disappeared inside the library, hoping that he
hadn't seen her.

With all that she's been through, Ellie's fortitude and
courage was now being tested in ways she never imagined, but if she were asked, there would be no question

in her mind that she would prevail because she possessed the strength of innocence. However, back in the North Pole, Santa Claus was also being tested. It was a different sort of test, of course, but a test nonetheless, and he was failing miserably. His love for his daughter and his commitment to her happiness and safety had made him happy and fulfilled. Yet, unlike Ellie, Santa was encumbered by his vast experience of the world, and it was this knowledge that now filled his mind with the overwhelming possibilities that could cause his daughter harm, and he remained paralyzed with fear. The weaknesses of adulthood haunted him, and rather than prevail, Santa's spirit turned blacker than his belt. He lost massive amounts of weight and continued to stand surrounded by the seals in the middle of the frozen tundra of the North Pole, screaming into the howling, blizzarding wind for the safe return of his Ellie.

A resigned Harry felt Santa's anguish from behind the kitchen window. He let the shades fall back into place, and with a heavy heart, he turned and faced Mrs. Claus.

"I don't know, Mrs. You can dip my tongue into the frozen Arctic for saying this, but I don't think we're going to make Christmas this year."

Charlotte turned away, deep in thought.

※

## TWENTY-SIX

Looking ruffled from running and feeling feverish and sweaty from all the clothes she was still wearing, Ellie walked into the massive nave of the library. She stared at all the women working behind the desks, but she didn't see her mother there, so she sauntered into the research area and immediately stopped. Ellie saw *her*, and she instantly reached into her pocket for the photograph, but she didn't pull it out because she knew right away. "My mother," she whispered.

She remained still, watching her mother peer through her reading glasses as she flipped through a book, then jotted down a note on a little piece of white paper and handed it to an elderly lady, who thanked her as she walked away. Lucy closed the book, picked up another, and began absentmindedly perusing the pages, when suddenly she stopped, pausing as if she sensed something. Lucy stared into Ellie's eyes, but Ellie broke from her gaze and walked slowly, carefully, toward her until she stopped in front of Lucy's desk.

"Excuse me," Ellie said, her voice breaking in bits and pieces.

"May I help you?" Lucy asked hesitantly.

Ellie fidgeted, then said more evenly, "Yes, I'm looking for books about . . ." She stopped mid-sentence as she suddenly became aware of her mother's penetrating eyes studying her face.

Ellie paused, then she stared back at her mother's face, noticing her eyes, soft and caring, the slight creases around her nose and chin, seeing the world, and feeling as if she'd known this woman for a thousand years. The silence between them ran long and deep until Lucy broke the trance and asked: "Yes . . . ?"

"I'm looking for books about Santa Claus," Ellie said, tearing her eyes away as she completed her thought.

"Santa Claus . . . ?" Lucy asked, puzzled.

"Yes, Santa Claus, of course."

Lucy thought for a second, then pointed. "Third aisle down on your right. Top shelf. He's under 'Myths and Fables.' "

"Why would you stick him there? He's not a myth or a fable," Ellie replied quickly. Then she felt odd, not for being quick and perhaps even sharp with her reply, but for defending Santa, with whom she was still very angry.

"He's not?"

"Nope," Ellie replied confidently. "May I read a few?"

"Well, umm . . . if you'd like, why don't you have a seat over there. I can pull a few books down for you. You'll never reach."

"Thanks." Ellie walked over to the reading table and sat, and a second later a large book dropped with a thud in front of her.

"According to this book, he was the Bishop of Myra during the fourth century," said Lucy.

"That's right," said Ellie, looking up. "He saved the lives of a couple of little boys from a bad man. That's how it all started."

Lucy dropped another book and Ellie quickly flipped through it.

"Oh, yeah, this one is all about his life in the Middle Ages. It was a tough time, you know, but that's when he made his move to the North Pole. He's been happy ever since. Well, until . . ."

And Lucy dropped yet another tome, saying, "Santa is the patron saint of Greece?"

"You bet, and he's real proud of that," Ellie said smiling.

And Lucy dropped more and more books on the table.

"Sinterklass in Holland . . ." BANG.

"Père Noël in France . . ." BAM.

"St. Nic in Russia . . ." BAM, BAM, BAM.

"Sinterklass in Finland and Norway, and Santa Claus in America." BAM, BAM, BAM! And Lucy collapsed in exhaustion into the chair next to Ellie.

Ellie eyed her mother. "You don't believe in him, do you?"

Lucy paused. "I don't think so . . ."

"Well, if he doesn't exist, then why are there so many books written about him?"

"I don't know . . . ," Lucy confessed softly.

"What about the North Pole? Do you believe in that?"

But instead of saying anything, Lucy looked at Ellie with wonder. . . .

"The reindeer?" persisted Ellie, and without waiting for an answer asked, "And what about the Christmas seals?"

"My husband always believed . . ."

"What about Mrs. Claus?"

"Yes . . . Please . . . I don't know . . . Who are you?" Lucy finally asked in frustration.

"If you believe in him," continued Ellie, "if it's in your heart, then anything can happen. Anything can come true."

Lucy's eyes welled with tears and she was about to grab this little girl, hug her with all her might and not let go—never let go again, never, ever; this beautiful child before her had to be hers—a mother knows—My God, she was about to cry, My baby, my beautiful baby has come back to me! and a tear fell from her eye. She leaned forward and Ellie's expectant eyes begged her to hold her, hold me, please, hold me real tight and never, ever let me go again—when all of a sudden Ellie saw, out of the corner of her eye, Peter lurking behind some shelves, and she immediately jumped out of her chair and screamed: "We have to go!"

"Wait, where!?"

"Your house! Can we go there!?" Ellie asked urgently.

"I guess . . . What's wrong?!" said Lucy, bewildered, knocking all the books off the table.

"Doesn't matter, just LET'S GO!"

And she grabbed Lucy's hand and dragged her away, barely giving Lucy a chance to snatch up her coat from her desk.

Peter jolted out from behind the shelves just in time to see their backs as they ran out the door. He took off, tripped on the books that lay on the floor, crashed into a book cart, fell to the ground, then quickly scampered back to his feet and chased after them.

It was all a blur as Lucy and Ellie raced for what seemed to be their lives past people and cars, street lamps and mailboxes. They ran with speed and abandon, and they felt invincible as they moved as one, because no one was going to catch them now. They dodged across the street just in time to reach out and grab the bus door from closing. With a sudden rush of air, it whipped back open and Ellie and Lucy boarded the bus, threw some coins at the driver, then ran to the back and dove into their seats, where they collapsed from exhaustion. The doors slammed shut and the bus coughed and spit, then it rumbled away from the curb and down Fifth Avenue. We're safe, thought Ellie, and she breathed in deeply. But then her anxiety returned and she propped herself up and pressed her face against the back window. She saw Peter jump into his hansom cab and quickly pull into the traffic, only to be caught behind a broken-down jalopy, which triggered a snarling traffic jam, and Peter was left behind waving his arms, yelling at the cars and trucks to get out of his way. Good! she thought.

Relieved, Ellie slid back down into her seat and looked up to Lucy saying calmly, "We're okay now."

Not knowing what had just happened and why, Lucy was nonetheless grateful and she reached over and grabbed little Ellie's hand.

## TWENTY-SEVEN

Harry walked somberly into the big room where the elves and regulars sat on their work stools, their hands cupped under their chins, staring catatonically at the candy-caned clock as the seconds and minutes ticked closer to eleven o'clock, Christmas Eve. The ramps weren't moving, the ovens weren't on, there was no rejoicing, there was no fun. In a word, it all seemed over. With nothing he could do, Harry shook his head and shuffled out of the room.

Peter's hansom cab was now swarming with barking, bleating, squawking dogs, cats, squirrels, and birds, a couple of wild rabbits, and even an owl or two, all arguing and fighting amongst themselves over how best to proceed with their search. Dorothy whinnied the loudest and proclaimed, "We need my friend, Man O' War, he can save the day! That's what I say!"

The other animals groaned.

"You know, he wanted me for his bride . . . I was quite the catch in my day. He just loved my ankles . . ." And Peter was certain Dorothy was losing her mind. But she wasn't finished, carrying on and on about her days back in Kentucky, until Peter screamed: "Quiet!" And everyone fell instantly silent.

"We're running out of time. Now stop the bickering and, please, will someone tell me which way should we go?!"

The animals looked at each other, then one by one, they started jabbering loudly again, until a little mouse crawled up Peter's arm, all the way up to his shoulders, where it stood on its two hind legs and with its little hands hanging on to Peter's ear, the mouse started to squeak in whispers until Peter's eyes popped open and he screamed: "How do we get there?! Quick, tell me! What's the fastest way!?" The animals screamed and yelled out the answer, and with a surge of energy, Peter grabbed the reins, knocking the poor little mouse off his shoulders and high into the air, and everyone stopped and watched as the little mouse unintentionally performed a triple somersault, then a double-sault, then a single-sault, finally ending with a classic double-gainer with a half-screw twist, only to land safely on the back of old Dorothy, who kicked her front legs up in the air and shot out into the street like a rocket, screaming: "GET THAT ROTTEN LITTLE FREELOADING MOUSE OFF MY BACK!"

❄

Ellie and Lucy slowly climbed the stairs to her apartment. They stopped in front of her door, and as Lucy fumbled through her purse looking for her keys, Ellie saw the small Christmas tree lying on its side in the corner of the hallway. She walked over and picked it up.

"Why'd you throw this out?" asked Ellie.

"It's silly," said Lucy. "I gave up on the whole Christmas season. . . ." And she opened the door and walked in.

Disappointed but not deterred, Ellie dragged the tree into the apartment, closing the door quickly behind her.

Then looking Lucy directly in her eyes, she smiled and said, "But you need this, because good things happen when you have it."

Lucy froze in shock. She had heard the same phrase, *"Good things happen when you have it!"* once before. She had heard it from Peter and it now echoed in her head, first in Peter's voice, then in the little girl's, floating in and out, over and over, crisscrossing until the voices melded together and became one and she was overwhelmed. She walked slowly, her hands reaching out to Ellie, their fingers touching until Lucy held her hands tight, leaned down and said, cautiously, "For eleven years, I put up little Christmas trees, believing, hoping, that I'd receive a gift, some sign . . . that my little girl was . . ."

"Safe . . . I know . . . I know everything . . . ," Ellie said, and Lucy began to tremble.

"How do you . . . are you . . . ?" Lucy stammered, still unsure she was able to confront reality.

Ellie walked away from her, went to the window, pulled the curtains to the side, and to her horror, she saw Peter in his hansom cab pull up and stop across the street. He jumped out and as he looked up to the building, Ellie whipped the curtains shut and turned to Lucy.

"I have something for you . . . ," Ellie said quickly, and she reached into her pocket and pulled out the crumpled note. She handed it slowly to Lucy, who opened it and her hands began to shake as she recognized her own handwriting. She twisted and turned her head away, unable to read or even look at Ellie, because she knew deep in her soul what the paper meant. The tears welled in her eyes and her whole body began to tremble, until slowly, her soul came back alive and she felt her heart beat for the first time in eleven years. Lucy faced her daughter, because it was true—it's *all true*— My daughter, this is my little Ellie and my sweet little girl has come back to me. She dropped to her knees, pulling her child deep into her bosom and cried out: "My God, my little girl is alive and well! You've come back to me!"

Sobbing with joy, she couldn't let go and she laid her head on the child's chest, saying, "I'm so sorry, so very sorry."

"It's okay, I found you," said Ellie, now crying too.

"We're together again."

"That's right, Mommy."

Lucy picked her head up and looked into her daughter's eyes. "Mommy . . . I never heard you say it before. You were just a baby. 'Mom.' 'Mommy.' Say it again! Please, say it again," she begged. "Mommy." And the sound of that precious word, "Mommy," rolled off her lips over and over again, until little Ellie said it—softly, sweetly, and Lucy's heart swelled with happiness.

"Oh, my little Ellie . . . Ellie . . . I love you . . ."

She relaxed her embrace and held Ellie at arm's distance, looking at her child as if for the first time, and Ellie thought she was looking at the prettiest woman she had ever seen.

"My God, where have you been? Are you okay? Don't we have to let the people you've been with know where you are?" she said, wiping the tears from her eyes with the back of her hand. "How'd you get here? Oh God, there's so much . . ."

There was much to ask, and since Lucy wanted to know everything instantly, her mind became jumbled with questions, but that quickly changed when she suddenly became aware of herself. Realizing she was a mother again—no longer alone to wallow in her thoughts and dreams, but a mother who must now take care of her child, and the responsibilities of that filled her with nervous energy and she quickly rose to her feet.

"Are you hungry? Let me fix you something to eat. Are you thirsty, can I get you anything . . . Oh dear, the icebox is empty."

So she ran into the kitchen, opening and closing the cupboards, the icebox, looking for something to give to her baby.

"Maybe later, okay, Mom," Ellie said simply.

Lucy stopped, brushed her hair back with her hands, and tried to calm down.

"Yes, yes, that's fine, maybe later." And she smiled at Ellie.

"Do you want to sit? We can talk."

Ellie turned away and walked back to the window, where she saw Peter still across the street, pacing, looking at his watch.

Ellie gritted her teeth, thinking, Why won't he leave me alone?

She turned back around, smiled at her mom, then sat down on the couch. Her nervous legs dangled above the floor.

"You have a lot of animals. I like that," Ellie said as she looked around the apartment and Lucy smiled sadly.

"Your father," she said as she looked down and fumbled with her fingers. "He was going to be a veterinarian."

"When I grow up, I'm going to be one too. My friend, he was going to be a vet, but then he . . ." Ellie stopped and she asked, "What was my dad like?"

Lucy walked to the couch and sat down, taking Ellie's hands in hers.

"He was a special man," she began, softly and gently. "Gracious and caring. He saw the goodness in everything." She paused, then said, "He died trying to save a little boy. He never knew you, never even knew I was going to have you . . ."

Silence.

"Ellie . . . ?"

"Yes, Mom."

"I need you . . . Can you stay?" Lucy asked with hope in her voice.

"I'm not going back," Ellie replied emphatically, and Lucy beamed.

"Ellie, sweetheart, can you tell me where you've been?"

"Up in the North Pole. Santa and Mrs. Claus raised me."

"Ellie, sweetie. Tell me, sweetheart, tell me all about the family that took care of you."

"I just did."

"I know, you said Santa and Mrs. Claus. But really, I think maybe we should call them. I'm sure they're worried."

"You can't call the North Pole," Ellie said matter-of-factly.

Lucy fidgeted. "Silly me, that's right," she said, trying to make light of the situation. "I know you can't call them, because, well . . . Santa and Mrs. Claus . . . don't exist."

"Yes, they do. They raised me."

Lucy didn't know what to make of this, but she was certain she should tread lightly.

"Ellie, dear . . . ," she began, in a tone of voice meant to subtly, hopefully, prompt Ellie to stop kidding around and tell the truth.

"You don't believe me," Ellie said, upset.

"Well, yes, I mean, no . . . ," Lucy said, fumbling.

"I'm not a liar," Ellie said, and she grew frustrated and disappointed that her mother didn't believe her. Then her thoughts switched to Peter. She was worried he would do something stupid, so she jumped off the couch, ran to the window to check on him, and he was gone! Her heart stopped. She shrieked, "Oh no, oh no!"

Lucy jumped off the couch. "Ellie, dear, what's the matter?!"

But Ellie didn't have time to answer. She was too busy thinking of a plan. We'd better run again, she thought, and she ran to another window, whipped back the shades, looked down the street from a different angle, but Peter was still missing.

Lucy had no idea what was happening. "Ellie, please, why do you keep looking out the window? Are the people who raised you, are they following you?"

For the last time, Ellie looked out the window. She spun around, and blurted, "There's a bad man. He wants to take me back. I don't want to go back. I want to stay with you so we have to go NOW!"

She ran for the door, but Lucy jumped in front of her, trying to hug her tight.

"It's okay," she said soothingly, "no one is going to hurt you . . ."

But Ellie wiggled away, and as she dove for her coat, they heard a knock at the door! Ellie cupped her mouth with her hands and took a couple of steps back.

"Don't open it," she pleaded.

"Why?" said Lucy, deeply troubled. "What's happening?"

Ellie didn't answer, instead, she just shook her head in fear.

Another knock!

Lucy looked at Ellie, then walked toward the door.

"Don't. Please!"

"It's going to be okay," Lucy comforted. "I have to talk to them." She opened the door and instantly fainted upon seeing Peter standing there.

Ellie ran over.

"Now look what you have done!" she railed, as she crouched down to her mother, trying her best to revive her.

Peter stood motionless, shocked, for he didn't know what to say, what to do. He had just seen his wife, the woman he died loving, and now, he was staring at his *daughter*—the daughter he never knew he had.

"You hurt her! You hurt my *mother*. This is my real mother!" she yelled as the tears welled in her eyes.

Peter crouched down, checked Lucy's breathing, and seeing she was fine, he then looked directly into Ellie's eyes.

"I know," he replied softly.

"Then go back to the North Pole and tell them I'm staying," she said, crying in fear of being taken away from her mother again.

"Ellie . . ."

"Go already!" she said, stamping her feet.

He took her hands. "Ellie, she was my wife."

"What!?" and she pulled away from him.

"Ellie, your mother, Lucy . . . was my wife," he repeated slowly.

The confusion in her mind started to turn to unidentifiable sounds.

"I . . . don't . . . I don't understand . . ."

"Oh, Ellie . . . ," he said, barely able to talk. "Ellie, you're my daughter."

"NO!" she screamed, and she jumped up and ran to the other side of the room.

"No! You're Peter. You're a regular, like the elves, like all the others."

"I didn't know. Honest, I didn't," said Peter, and he pulled from his pocket the crystal snowflake pendant. "I bought this for your mother on Christmas Eve, eleven years ago. Before I knew we were going to have you. She must have given it to you when she . . ."

Now the sounds of confusion became a frightening rush of white noise and she grabbed her head and yelled.

"You're a mean man and you'll say anything to bring me back to the North Pole!"

He took a hesitant step toward her. "No, please . . . I have always loved you . . ."

"You're lying. Stay away from me! You're crazy! You can't be my father!"

Blinded by her tears and choked with anger, she sprinted past Peter, who tried to grab her. But Ellie scooted under Peter's arms and ran out of the door.

Peter quickly dropped to his knees, cradled Lucy in his arms, and gently patted her cheeks until—her eyes shot open and she instinctively called out, "Ellie!"

"It's me, my love," he whispered.

She focused her eyes and looked at him in disbelief. "Peter . . . ?"

"Yes, it's me," he said, and he kissed her deeply, and she thought she was dreaming, floating through time, remembering, then reliving their first kiss, against the tree in front of her house, when the sun had just dropped under the horizon and the sky turned orange and blue, feeling for the first and only time in her life the glorious wonder of becoming one with someone else. Their lips parted and Peter said with urgency, "We don't have much time!"

"How . . . ?" Lucy asked, still in shock.

"I'll explain later, but let's just say I was right about the North Pole."

"My God . . . Ellie said the same thing. What's going on . . . ?"

"Santa saved her."

"Stop. What are you saying? I don't understand . . ."

"Ellie's been with me ever since . . . Please, Lucy, trust me. We have to go now!" He pulled his wife to her feet.

"Why . . . ? Where's Ellie?!" she persisted, desperately trying to make sense of it all.

"She ran away. She doesn't believe me and I only have fifteen minutes left . . ."

"What!?"

He quickly grabbed her hand and they charged out of the apartment.

## TWENTY-EIGHT

It was all too much for Ellie to bear and with tears streaming down her face she ran through the streets. First her mother and now her . . . father? All those years together in the North Pole and Peter never said anything? Santa and Mrs. Claus lied to me. I have no friends anymore.

She turned the corner, and just as she disappeared into a long alley, Peter and Lucy charged out of Lucy's building and jumped into the waiting hansom cab chock full of animals.

"Let's go, Dorothy," Peter commanded as he grabbed the reins.

Dorothy whinnied, saying, "And what's the magic word?"

Peter, along with all the other animals, screamed: "PLEASE!"

But hats off to cranky ol' Dorothy, because she put aside her problems and summoned all her strength and she took off galloping down the street with speed and grace, just like her friend Man O' War.

"Yah!" thundered Peter, and everyone held on tight.

❄

Back inside Santa's house, Harry, Kid Twist, Nutter, and Mrs. Claus peered through the frosted kitchen windows and saw Santa with his suit hanging off his emaciated looking body, still screaming into the howling wind.

They stepped away from the windows, and looked at the clock. It read: 11:45 P.M.

"So . . . anyone got any ideas? And I mean big ones, not little ones. Big ones," Harry said.

"He's getting really thin," remarked Twist.

"That's not an idea!" Harry shouted.

"We're never going to make it," said Nutter.

"No kidding," replied Harry.

Shaking with nerves, Kid Twist looked at the clock. "And Peter's only got fifteen minutes left."

Grim, Harry stole a quick look at Mrs. Claus, then turned away saying, "It doesn't look good for him, Mrs."

But Charlotte wasn't listening to him. Instead, she was hearkening to her inner voice, which started as a whisper, then grew to the sound of a thousand trumpets blaring the name over and over again: "Peter . . . PETER! . . . That's it!"

"What's *it?!*" asked Harry, confused, as he watched Charlotte jump to her feet and put on her coat.

"Just start cooking some food, and I mean a lot of food. I'll be right back," she said, and with that, she was out the door, leaving Harry, Twist, and Nutter with nothing better to do than stare at each other with dumbfounded expressions.

"Well, you heard the Mrs.," shouted Harry. "Let's start cooking!"

Before Harry even finished wiping the sweat from his brow, Twist and Nutter had jumped to their feet, and in a flash, whipped open the refrigerator door; and the next thing Harry knew, eggs and large roasts, veal chops and steaks, great slabs of ham and pies flew out of the refrigerator and around the room a couple of times, only to land magically on all the plates already set on the table.

Surprised but pleased, Harry smiled, thinking, Well, just stick some ice chips in my eyes! I didn't know they could do that.

❈

Dorothy had slowed down to a flimsy trot and Peter and Lucy were losing hope. All the animals sat low in their seats looking defeated.

"We're running out of time," Peter said nervously.

"Why do you keep saying that?!" asked Lucy.

"Where could she be?" replied Peter.

"Wait. Let me think," said Lucy.

"She doesn't know the city," said Peter. Then it dawned on him. "Mrs. Hardwick's. I saw her there. She was looking for you."

"Go. Go," said Lucy, and Peter pulled at the reins and Dorothy snorted, then trotted as fast as she could toward the evil Hardwick's.

## TWENTY-NINE

Ellie ran through the streets as if chased by demons. Faster still she ran, until she put her head down and all she saw through the tears in her eyes was the whirling blur of her feet and the dark gray ground disappearing fast underneath her. She ran from it all, leaving nothing behind but the little puffs of her breath hitting the cold air. Dizzy, she looked up and suddenly realized she was there. She charged up the stairs of the old dilapidated building and knocked hard on the door. No answer. She knocked again! Still no answer. Desperate, Ellie ran down the stairs, thinking she would find a rock or a piece of coal to throw through the— No, all the windows were broken, what good was that going to do? She twisted around, not knowing where to go next, when suddenly, the front door swung open and this time for good, as it flew off the hinges and tumbled off the stoop and down the stairs, and standing unsteadily inside the empty door frame with a half-empty bottle of booze swinging in one hand was Mrs. Hardwick.

"Got some money for me?" she growled.

"I have nowhere to go," pleaded Ellie.

"That makes two of us. Come on in." She waved Ellie over, and without a second's hesitation, little Ellie dashed up the stairs, over the broken door, and with one great jump hurled herself inside the tenement. Impressed, Hardwick nodded, then leaned to grab the door, but since it wasn't there, she stumbled forward, and almost fell on her face. With disgust, she waved her hand at the door and walked inside.

"This way," she said as she walked past Ellie, who stood in the shadows of the dark hallway. Ellie followed Hardwick, who held a lit candle in her hand, up the first flight of stairs, then the second, creaking and groaning after each step, all the way to the top floor, where she unlocked her door and they entered what Hardwick called home. Others, however, would be correct in calling it seedy and squalid, or even grubby and mucky. And some might even go out on a limb and call it polluted and foul. But most would say it was a musty, filthy, mice-ridden empty-bottle depository with clothes all over the floor, dirty dishes stacked to the ceiling, and a bunch of broken-up furniture collecting dust by the small fireplace in the corner of the room.

Ellie called it a dump with a cat and a scrawny parrot.

Hardwick put the candle down on top of the dresser, then threw some pieces of broken furniture into the fire and it roared alive. Ellie took off her coat and sweater and looked for a clean place to put it down—so she held on to her things. The parrot chirped.

"I thought you ate the parrot," said Ellie.

"I did. That's another one your mother left. I kept it because it drops an egg every once in a while. I eat those. And, see," she said smiling, "I got a kitty-cat here for you to play with."

It was really a tomcat, but Ellie decided not to correct her. Instead, she watched as Hardwick hunched her back and stumbled through the apartment calling, "Here, kitty-kitty, here kitty . . . I just want to give you a little pet . . . maybe wring your neck. . . . Here kitty . . ." She finally cornered the tom, lunged for it, but the cat hissed and scooted away.

"Damn cat is nasty, but at least it eats all the mice," she said as she straightened out her back and hydroplaned a mouthful of booze down her throat.

"You need to pet it," said Ellie as she put her hand out for the tom to lick, which he did, and in exchange for that favor the tom allowed Ellie to pick him up and pet his back until he purred.

"See," said Ellie, putting the cat back down.

"Like I care," said Hardwick and she plopped herself down on a beat-up chair and drank.

"So what happened? Your mother didn't want you back? I knew she was a no-good deadbeat."

"No, she's not and that's not nice!"

"Here we go again," Hardwick said, waving her hands in the air. "Then what's the ticket?"

"My dad. He wants to take me back to the North Pole."

"Whattaya talking about? Your dad's dead. Croaked years ago." Hardwick kicked at the cat with her feet.

"Not really. He lives in the North Pole with me and Santa."

Hardwick eyed Ellie, then got up and poured some of her brandy into the fire. WHOOSH!

"I think I'm drinking too much."

Just then, the tom rubbed its back against her leg, and Hardwick, still smarting from being rejected by the ingrate, quickly leaned down, grabbed it by the back of its neck, raised it up to her drunken eyes, and screamed, "Get away from me!" The tom hissed at her, and with the cat still firmly in her hand, she spun around like a discus thrower, then flung it with all her might across the room—"Yeowwwww!" Hardwick, drunk and dizzy, fell off balance, twirled around and dropped like a stone, hitting her head hard against the fireplace brick.

"Hey!" shouted Ellie, and she ran across the room to catch the flying tom, but it was too late. The cat crashed into the dresser on the other side of the room, knocking the candle against the dusty curtains hanging down by the windows and—WHOOSH!

The flames flew up the fabric, then onto the walls,

and within seconds the whole place was an inferno. Ellie froze in horror.

"Mrs. Hardwick!"

She ran to the old drunk and started pulling at her arms and legs, anything to get her up and out of there.

## THIRTY

Pulling her coat tight around her neck, Mrs. Claus charged out to the frozen tundra, where Santa, thinner than ever, still stood screaming for his baby to come home.

"Santa!" she called out through the wind as she continued to march toward him.

"I want my Ellie!" he cried, his voice weak from yelling and hunger.

"Get off the tundra and into the house right now!" she demanded.

"I'm tired, Charlotte. I'm not going. Without Ellie I don't see the reason."

Charlotte was now close enough to reach out and grab her husband. She shook his shoulders.

"Don't you say that. Ever!" she said. Then she pounded his chest with her fists and when she was finished, she took a step back and said, "There are millions of other children, waiting, depending on you, not just for a gift, but to restore a belief in them that there is *still* some hope, goodness, and compassion in this world. And they deserve just one day out of the year to wake up and be happy and not think about some war or worry about their parents fighting because there's no food on the table." She paused and then said softly, "It is not just about our child, Santa. It's about *all the children.*"

"I used to believe that," he said, now facing her.

"Well, there's something else."

"What?"

She took a breath, and the cold air burned her lungs.

"Peter is Ellie's father."

Santa stiffened and his once-red face was now as white as his beard.

Charlotte continued.

"I fought it in my heart, but I'm sure . . ."

"No . . . ," he said almost in a whisper.

"I knew when he first saw her, eleven years ago. I saw it in his eyes."

"Charlotte . . . don't, please."

"The way they held hands, played, and laughed at the same things. It was deep in their soul . . ."

"They were just friends . . ."

"It was more than that. The day Ellie left, she threw away the crystal snowflake pendant her mother had given her. Peter found it. It was the same pendant Peter gave to his wife the day he died."

"Lots of people . . ."

"No, Santa . . . I'm certain because . . . because . . ."
And she stopped. She was crying too hard.

"Why, Charlotte, tell me."

She wiped the tears from her face. "Because Peter's
not going to return in time."

"It can't be," he said in disbelief. "None of this can
be . . . how?" He searched her face, hoping she would
tell him it was all a mistake.

"Because, dear, because, my sweet foolish husband,
Peter would rather turn into a comet than forsake his
daughter. Don't you understand? He won't give up. He's
willing to give his life until he's sure that she's safe and
protected down there and *only a father* would do that."

"What have I done?" he said, collapsing to the frozen
ground.

Charlotte got down on her knees with him, took his
hands into hers.

"You have to save him," she pleaded. "Make the
exception. Please, Santa, save him, save the children.
You have the power to do it. Now is the time."

"Do you think?"

"Oh, God, yes, Santa. Yes."

He stared into her beautiful, forgiving face and he
knew she was right. My God, he loved her, and he kissed
her lips hard and then got up and ran as fast as he could
toward the kitchen, because, well . . . he was very hungry, but the real reason was this: Santa knew what he
had to do, and for that, he was going to need all the
energy he could get.

# THIRTY-ONE

The ravenous flames ate away at Hardwick's apartment, picking it clean with their whipping tongues and teeth, then showing its gratitude by spitting out some black ash. Frantic, Ellie hovered over Mrs. Hardwick, slapping her face harder and harder until Hardwick's eyes opened.

"We have to go!" screamed Ellie.

Hardwick finally jumped up and together they ran for the front door, but a flaming beam fell in front of them, blocking their path. They spun around, ran toward the back, then Ellie remembered the cat and she pulled away from Hardwick, jumped over a pile of burning clothes and wood, pushed the dresser to the side, and grabbed the tomcat, still unconscious but alive. With the cat safely cradled in one arm, she ran back to Hardwick, picking up the parrot cage as she went, then coughing and wheezing, she managed to hand the cage to Hardwick. Together, they ran for the back door and escaped into the hallway, only to be met by thick smoke and more flames. They dropped to their knees and felt the heat rising from the floor, and ever so carefully, they placed the palms of their hands down against the floor, only to quickly pull them back up—too hot. Having no choice, they covered their mouths the best they could, and duckwalked down the hall toward the staircase that would hopefully lead them to the roof.

❋

Twist and Nutter did cartwheels and back flips when they saw Santa running from the tundra toward the kitchen door. Harry ran to the window, pressed his face against the frosted glass, and with his own eyes saw him coming too.

He slapped his thighs and shouted, "Well, how about them candied apples!?" Jumping up and down with excitement, Twist and Nutter climbed up on his shoulders, happily slapping Harry's back, rubbing his head and hair, giving him little noogies; and for the first time in Harry's life up in the North Pole, he silently admitted to himself how much he actually enjoyed their affection, and he smiled widely.

"Santa's back!" they all shouted and Harry danced a jig, slowly at first then all around the kitchen, and Twist and Nutter, still perched on his shoulders, held on tight;

but as Harry danced faster and wilder, the two elves started to rock back and forth until they couldn't hold on any longer and they crashed to the ground.

The kitchen door slammed open and Santa stood there, staring curiously at Twist and Nutter sprawled on the floor. Then he looked at the smiling Harry and he thought that was unusual as well, but right now, he couldn't be bothered with the whole question and answer routine, so he barked, "Harry! Get my gold sack!" and then he dove for the table. He didn't bother picking up the forks or knives, didn't even think about wrapping his big linen napkin around his neck, nope, Santa just put his hands underneath the platters of turkey, roast beef, and pies and lifted them up to his mouth, and within minutes, the food was pretty much gone.

Harry didn't move and he stared at Santa not because he was amazed at how quickly the food disappeared. No. He stood in shock because he had heard Santa say: "Get my gold sack."

Santa looked up, pulled the turkey leg out of his mouth and said, with a gleam in his eye, "You know what I'm talking about, Harry. I *need* the gold sack."

Harry nodded slowly . . .

"Well then," said Santa, "you'd better hurry it up, we don't have much time."

Finally, Harry sprung to life, snapped his suspenders against his chest, and ran out of the kitchen, prompting Santa to remark: "That's the first time I've seen Harry run in over a hundred years."

✳

"We're there, we're there," whinnied Dorothy, exhausted and cranky. "I've got calcium deposits all over my feet now, and visions of the glue factory are dancing in front of my eyeballs, but we're there!"

"Almost, pal. Just around the corner. You'll make it," said Peter tensely. He looked over to Lucy and took her hand in his and all the animals stood on their hind feet, then clasped their little hands together, hoping and praying they would find Ellie. With barely any energy left in her legs, Dorothy turned the corner and Lucy screamed out: "Oh my God!"

They all stared in horror at the flames engulfing Hardwick's tenement. Peter and Lucy howled: "GO! GO! GO! DOROTHY! THAT'S IT! DON'T WORRY, ELLIE! WE'RE COMING!"

Wasting no time, Dorothy kicked up her front legs and shot like a racehorse down the block, then right in front of Hardwick's apartment, her front two legs locked, her hooves dug into the street, and she leaned back with all her might and they stopped.

Peter and Lucy jumped out of the cab and looked up and saw—

"Ellie!" yelled Lucy.

Up on the roof, Ellie, still clutching the tom against her chest, stood frightened and shaking next to Hardwick, who was swinging the parrot cage like a lantern, as they both cried: "HELP!"

Lucy cupped her mouth with her hands and yelled again, "Don't worry, my love, we're going to save you!"

Ellie looked down crying: "Help! Mom! Peter! Help!"

"We're burning up!" shouted Mrs. Hardwick.

"We're coming!" answered Peter.

"Ellie!" wailed Lucy, and Peter quickly tore off his coat.

"I'm going in," he said with determination.

"But you'll never make it," screamed Lucy in a panic.

"Neither one of us will if I don't," he shouted back. "It's our only chance!" He raced toward the missing front door, threw the coat over his head, and in one leap, landed at the top of the stairs, where he quickly disappeared inside the burning building.

"Hurry, Peter! Hurry!" Lucy cried.

"MOM!" yelled Ellie.

"Call the firemen!" yelled Mrs. Hardwick.

"Help, please, come quick. The flames are coming up to our feet!" cried Ellie.

"Hold on, Ellie! Help is coming!"

Peter fought his way up the burning staircase, choking and coughing from the smoke. The flames, now insatiably hungry for everything, licked and lapped at him, nipping at his arms, his hair, and face with its tongue, sampling his taste and deciding he would be a good addition to the feast. Suddenly, a flaming beam collapsed and Peter dove under it, scampering back to his feet and charging back up the stairs heading for the roof—where the flames were now creeping toward Ellie and Hardwick. They spun in fear, pinning themselves against the ledge of the roof, with nowhere else to go.

All at once, the flames tore through, eating whole sections with a single swipe, devouring great chunks of wood and tar. The roof shook and growled, fighting, straining, but ultimately conceding to the voracious flames, and it was now only a matter of time before the entire building collapsed within itself. Then it happened. The roof opened under her feet and little Ellie's arms flew up and she fell into a hole. Hardwick quickly reached out. Little Ellie was stuck, wedged between two beams.

"Oh my God! Ellie!!!!" screamed Lucy.

Hardwick leaned over and tried to pull her out of the hole, but she couldn't.

The flames were getting closer.

## THIRTY-TWO

Santa finished every last morsel of beef, turkey, fish, ham hocks, pies, and cookies and he washed it all down by guzzling a great canister of milk. Then with a flourish, he whipped the napkin off his neck and stood, revealing to Harry, Twist, Nutter, and Mrs. Claus that he was once again big and rolly. His face was flushed and red like his suit, and they all smiled with relief.

"Okay, this is what we're going to do," he announced. "Get everything ready, the presents, the lists, some snacks . . ."

"It's all on the sleigh," said Harry proudly.

"Take it off," ordered Santa, and Harry's shoulders slumped.

"You're the boss."

"All right, good. Now, I'll be back soon. Then you'll put everything on the sleigh and Mrs. Claus and I will fly together," he said, clapping his hands. "Now, give me the gold sack."

Harry placed a blue box with a gold lock on the table. He whipped out a little key from his vest pocket and unlocked it. He reached in and carefully pulled out the large gold sack, which glistened under the candlelight. It was clearly special and with great reverence he handed the sack to Santa, who turned, looked at his wife, then slung it over his back and shouted: "Come on, let's go, let's go! It's Christmas time!"

Excited and holding hands, Twist and Nutter sprinted toward the kitchen door, where they collided and ended up wedged inside the frame. With a quick shove, Harry pushed them through, making way for Santa to step over them. Then he was gone.

"I'd better get dressed," said Mrs. Claus excitedly, and she jumped over Nutter and Twist and disappeared.

Harry stood in the kitchen, scratching his head and mumbling: "I shoulda walked in the other direction."

❋

Dozens of fire trucks screeched to a stop in front of Hardwick's. The firemen jumped off, grabbed their hoses and ladders, and ran to the building, but then they stopped. The walls had already crumbled into leftovers for the flames to eat as dessert. Quickly deciding there was little they could do, they raced to the truck, pulled out a huge net, and ran back to the building, where they fanned out into a semicircle, spreading the net. They looked up and beseeched Hardwick to jump.

With the birdcage still swinging in her hand, she looked down at the firemen and screamed back: "Whattaya nuts?! I ain't jumping nowheres, and besides, LITTLE ELLIE IS STUCK!"

Lucy, standing helplessly down below, almost fainted. "Please save her, somebody! Where's Peter?!"

"Jump!" the fireman yelled back to Hardwick.

Hardwick spun back around, looked at Ellie, still stuck in the hole, then at the flames coming closer. She leaned over the ledge and saw the net, ready and waiting for her, and all she thought was, Darn, I could use a drink right about now. She turned back to Ellie and said, "Whattaya think, kid?"

With her head sinking lower under the collapsing roof and coughing harder from the relentless smoke billowing and swirling around her, Ellie knew there was nothing she could do and said, "It's okay. But take the cat."

Hardwick ran over, grabbed the cat, then said, "Sorry, but we're all square, right? . . . I mean, what's the sense of both of us turning into some well-done steak . . ."

She looked into little Ellie's forgiving eyes, then threw up her hands in frustration and said, "Ahhh hell, kid . . . I can't do this." She ran over to the ledge and flung the cat and the birdcage off the roof. "Yeeooow!" the cat screamed, but both the cage and the cat landed safely in the net. Hardwick leaned down and screamed: "I'm sticking with the kid!"

"Please help her!" implored Lucy.

"I'm trying!" Hardwick shot back, and just then Peter broke through the roof door, and jumping over great craters filled with flames, dove for little Ellie.

"PETER!" she cried, through her coughs.

"I'm here, my love!"

"I'm sorry, Peter, I'm really sorry."

Hardwick almost fainted. With her mouth barely moving said, "Look, pal—" speaking through the dark waves of smoke "—I really don't care if you're alive or dead, just save the kid!"

"Don't worry, but you'd better jump. I'll take care of her," he said.

"Whatever you say," Hardwick replied and with that she raced back to the ledge, climbed on top, and jumped.

Time was running out and Peter didn't have to look at his watch to see the minute hand ticking closer to midnight, he knew it. He reached into the hole and, with both hands, he started to pull little Ellie up.

"ELLIE!" screamed Lucy.

"Hurry, Peter," Ellie said weakly.

"Don't worry, I'll get you out quickly," he said as urgently as he could without scaring her, and slowly, slowly, pulling and straining, he tried to pull her out. But the smoke was overwhelming and Ellie coughed again. She was fading fast, but he managed to get one hand free—

"Stay with me, Ellie," he pleaded. "Stay with me!" Then the other hand came free, and within seconds, her whole body was lifted out of the hole. But Ellie was no longer conscious.

The clock ticked closer to midnight.

Peter hugged Ellie's inert body, then lifted her into his arms, pressed her close to his chest, and ran toward the ledge. He climbed up.

Seconds, seconds . . . away from . . .

"JUMP, JUMP!" Lucy screamed, as she saw a wall of fire rising and curling up behind them.

"JUMP!"

"JUMP ALREADY, FOR CRYIN' OUT LOUD!" screamed Hardwick.

The firemen waited down below, ready to catch them.

With Ellie cradled in his arms, Peter jumped, and the clock hit midnight!

And as they began to fall, Peter started feeling weak, then he sensed his whole body breaking down into molecules, and he screamed: "No! MY ELLIE!"

"What's happening?" asked Lucy.

"What the hell!?" Mrs. Hardwick added, watching in horror as Peter began to quickly disintegrate into bits and pieces of swirling chemicals and particles, atoms and protons, and Peter could no longer hold his daughter and she slipped through his fingers and started to free fall. Lucy and Hardwick ran to get under her, but the firemen were there with their net and she landed safely. Lucy lunged in and grabbed her daughter, but she saw that Ellie wasn't breathing.

"Oh, my God!" gasped Lucy.

Then she looked up and saw Peter, now a whirlpool of swirling molecules spinning together, forming a ball, indeed—a comet! And—WHOOSH!

He shot up into the sky and Lucy watched him disappear.

"Peter . . ."

With tears in her eyes, she quickly leaned down and started to resuscitate Ellie, breathing, breathing, with short little bursts into Ellie's mouth. Lucy whipped her head back and gasped for air.

"Oh, God! Please, Ellie!" she cried.

"Come on, kid!" urged Mrs. Hardwick and Lucy tried again. She breathed into Ellie's mouth, again and again, until little Ellie coughed softly, then her whole body shook from a series of heaving coughs, and before Ellie even opened her eyes, Lucy lifted her up and pulled her into her chest, and Ellie woke feeling her mother's warm embrace.

Old lady Hardwick, grateful that little Ellie made it, stood and watched her building crumble—the hungry flames now sated. She shook her head, smiled, and then said to no one in particular, "I'm never going to be nasty again."

# THIRTY-THREE

With a speed and force no man could ever match, Santa's sleigh flew straight into the heavens and within seconds he was flying among billions of stars. His cap flew off his head and his cherubic face was flattened from the extraordinary force, yet he gripped the reins with all his might and the reindeer responded. With their legs tucked tight under their torsos, they shot up like a rocket and zipped through the Milky Way, into the outer reaches of the galaxy where up ahead, Santa finally saw it, a comet, its tail leaving a wake of sparkling particles, racing to nowhere.

"On, Dancer! On, Vixen! On, Donner!" he screamed. All eight reindeer pointed their noses, closed their eyes, and shot even faster into the heavens. The sled was getting closer and closer to the comet, neck and neck, back and forth, racing through the heavens. Santa covered his eyes from the shower of particles whipping at him from the comet's tail. He cracked the reins one last time. It was now or never, and the reindeer inched ahead, then gained some more, and with one more crack of the reins, they were now speeding past the comet. Santa slowly, unsteadily stood up, then fell back down—they were moving way too fast. He tried again. With his knees wobbling, he stood, and with one hand he held on tight to the side railing, and with the other, he pulled out the special gold sack! He leaned out of the sleigh, his hair whipping in the wind, opened his sack wide, and BAM!

The comet flew right into it! Santa spun around and fell into the backseat of the sleigh. He took a deep breath, then with all his might, he pulled the sack onto his lap, patted it with both hands, leaned back, and started laughing with joy.

✳

## THIRTY-FOUR

The next morning, when they awakened in bed together, Lucy and Ellie rubbed the sleep from their eyes and walked slowly into the living room. They stood still and silent, heartbroken at the sight of the small barren Christmas tree, its needles flaking off, with no lights, no garlands, and worst of all, not even the smallest reminder of any kind under the tree that Santa or Peter had ever existed.

Their hands clasped together, they remained facing the tree. If there was any solace, it was the gratitude they had in their hearts for being with each other once again. They embraced, and after separating, Ellie turned back to the tree.

"Look!"

Lucy spun around, and before she knew it, the tree was draped with green garlands. POP! wrapped with strings of pearls. POP! POP! POP! hundreds of glistening ornaments hanging on every branch. POP! blinking lights everywhere. POP! A brilliant, bright white star appeared on top of the tree.

In a state of shock, Lucy and Ellie faced each other, only to be further astonished when they turned back around and saw Santa and Mrs. Claus standing next to the tree with two large sacks in their hands!

"Santa . . . ," Lucy said softly. Santa smiled warmly. Ellie looked at her mom, tugged at her sleeve, and asked, "Do you believe now?"

"Always," Lucy replied in a whisper, but the glorious moment was short-lived, as her instincts took over and she quickly grabbed Ellie's hand.

Mrs. Claus noticed.

"It's okay, Lucy," she said, reassuringly. "We're not here for Ellie."

"That's right," agreed Santa.

Lucy relaxed, ever so slightly.

"Santa and I . . . we've discussed this at great length," said Mrs. Claus.

"We did what we could, we did what we thought was right," said Santa, then he paused. "You see, I was the one who found Ellie crying in front of the orphanage. When I picked her up, she smiled, and for the first time in my long life, I knew what it felt like to be a father and it was the most glorious, complete feeling I ever had. I'm sorry, but I hope you understand."

"But it's over now," said Mrs. Claus. "It's time for Ellie to be with you . . ."

"That is, if she wants," said Santa with a coy smile and a quick wink to Ellie, who smiled back. Then Ellie looked up into the eyes of her mother, gave her a quick wink, then she squeezed her mother's hand tightly to confirm her love.

"Thank you," Lucy said to Santa and Mrs. Claus. "Thank you, Santa and Mrs. Claus, for taking care of my baby."

Then a silence fell over the room as Santa and Mrs. Claus struggled with their feelings.

"We brought you something," said Santa sweetly, leaning over to untie one of the bags, but the string was all mangled in knots.

"I don't want any presents," Ellie cried softly. "I wish Peter was here."

"Ellie . . . sweetheart," comforted Lucy.

"But we have something special," said Santa, still struggling with the string.

"No . . . no, thank you," said Lucy, putting up her hand for Santa to stop. "I saw my husband again . . . that was more than . . . it was more than a dream come true . . . and for a few beautiful minutes, the most cherished I have ever known, we were a family again. My daughter—" and her voice began to break "—my daughter is back. You gave this to us and I can't ask for anything more."

"I miss Peter . . . my dad," said Ellie crying.

Santa and Mrs. Claus looked at each other, then Santa pulled out a little penknife from inside his jacket, and cut the string with great fanfare—and out popped Peter!

Lucy covered her mouth in shock. Ellie raced to her father.

"PETER!" she cried as she fell into his opened arms and hugged him with everything she had.

Santa and the Mrs. smiled.

With Ellie's arms still wrapped around his neck, Peter craned his head over and looked Lucy in her eyes, which she closed, convincing herself that it was all real. Peter gently pulled Ellie's arms off his neck and handed her to Santa. He walked slowly toward his wife. Their hands reached out, and they stroked each other's face. Their lips came together and kissed, ever so softly . . . and then they embraced.

Santa coughed, coughed again, and Peter and Lucy separated.

"We have to go now," said Santa gently.

"Oh, my child . . . ," cried Mrs. Claus as she opened her arms for Ellie to run into. They hugged, then Ellie turned to Santa.

"Good-bye . . . Dad . . ."

"No, no, dear, no good-byes. And, sweetheart . . . ," he said as he dropped to his knees and held her hands. "From now on, you call me Santa. Because you see there," pointing to Lucy and Peter. "That's your mom and dad, your *real* mom and dad, and they were kind enough to let us be together for a little while . . . you're a lucky little girl, Ellie . . . look at all the people who love you." He leaned in and hugged her and for a moment; he wasn't sure if he could let go, so he hugged her tighter, until a tear fell from his eye and he knew it was time to leave.

He looked at her from an arm's distance and she said, "See you later, Santa."

"I like that. It sounds right," he said smiling. He leaned in and kissed her gently on her forehead.

"Love you . . . ," Ellie said to Mrs. Claus.

"Love you too, my sweet girl . . ." They hugged, then Ellie walked back to her parents and held their hands. There was an awkward pause, until Santa said these very quiet words: "Come on, Peter, it's time to go."

Sadly, Peter turned and looked at him.

"The rules . . . ?" Peter asked softly and Santa nodded, whispering under his breath, "Yes, the rules."

Peter looked down at Ellie and his eyes told her that he must leave her.

"Daddy! No! Don't go!" she cried. With his heart breaking, he quickly crouched down and pulled her into his chest.

"Sweetheart, I have to," he tried to explain.

"Please, Peter . . . You're supposed to . . . you're supposed to stay with us and be my daddy."

"Ellie . . . You'll be with your mom," he said with love in his voice as he looked at his wife. "And you will always be with me . . . right here, right in my heart," he said, patting his heart with his fist. He kissed her face. "And remember, my sweet girl, I love you and your mom . . . more than all the stars in the heavens." He began to cry.

"And I love you and Ellie more than all the snowflakes that have ever fallen," said Lucy.

Peter rose, walked to his wife, and they kissed. He took a step back, reached into his pocket, and took out the crystal snowflake pendant that he had wanted to give to her eleven years ago. He gently draped the jewel over Lucy's head. She held it in her hands, looked at Peter, and they embraced.

Ellie ran to them and wrapped her little arms around her mother and father, holding them tight, tighter, unwilling to let go.

Finally, Peter stepped away, walked to Santa and Mrs. Claus, turned and faced his family.

"I'll see you next year. Promise," he assured them.

Ellie couldn't bear it and she hid in her mother's arms and Lucy kissed her on her head, and when they both looked up again, Peter, Santa, and Mrs. Claus were gone.

"The roof!" Lucy exclaimed. They raced out of the apartment, through the halls and up the staircase leading to the roof. Ellie was first to burst through the door. Up in the sky she saw Peter in the front seat of the sleigh, silently guiding the magnificent and loyal eight. In the back, sat Santa and Mrs. Claus.

"Look, Mom," said Ellie pointing up to the sky. Lucy looked up and saw Santa snuggle closer to Mrs. Claus and then drape his arm around her shoulder. Mrs. Claus rested her head against his chest, gazing into her husband's eyes. Lucy remembered the times she did that with Peter and smiled.

"Okay, Peter," said Santa, "give us one more whirl around Manhattan and then we'd better go by George's place and get Rudolph."

Peter smiled and snapped the reins. The sleigh banked and swooped down back toward the roof. Standing under the starry Manhattan skyline, Ellie and Lucy waved good-bye to Peter, Santa, and Mrs. Claus zipping overhead, soaring high and away, until they slowly disappeared into the very—

Good night.

# Order this beautiful
# Christopher Radko glass ornament today!

# SPECIAL EXCLUSIVE OFFER!

With the purchase of *Little Ellie Claus* by James Manos, Jr., you can buy this beautifully designed glass Christmas ornament by Christopher Radko for only $21 (plus shipping and handling)!

## OFFICIAL MAIL-IN ORDER FORM
To receive your Christopher Radko ornament by mail,
### just follow these simple instructions:

❈ Purchase the hardcover edition of James Manos, Jr.'s *Little Ellie Claus* by January 31, 2001.

❈ Mail this official form (no photocopies accepted) and the proof of purchase (the original store receipt) for each book dated on or before January 31, 2001, with the purchase price of *Little Ellie Claus* circled.

❈ Send this form along with a $25.25 check or money order (includes $4.25 for postage and handling—please do not send cash or stamps). Make check payable to CHRISTOPHER RADKO PROMOTIONAL OFFER.

**I have enclosed a check or money order for $_____**

Offer good from November 1, 2000–February 28, 2001, or while supplies last. Mail in coupon, proof of purchase, and check or money order for $25.25, all of which must be received by February 28, 2001. All requests must be submitted with this original form. Offer valid only to individual consumers in the United States and District of Columbia. Offer not valid in Canada. Limit one (1) ornament per household. Offer void where prohibited, taxed, or otherwise restricted by law. Allow two weeks for delivery. Not responsible for late, lost, misdirected, incorrect, illegible, incomplete or postage-due mail. All submissions are subject to verification. Fraudulent submission could result in prosecution under federal mail fraud statutes. This product is not for resale and no retail returns or refunds are permissible.

Print your full address clearly for proper UPS delivery of your merchandise (no P.O. boxes, please—UPS cannot deliver to P.O. boxes):

Name _____

Street Address _____ Apt. #_____

City _____ State _____ Zip_____

Mail this completed form along with your proof of purchase and check or money order to:
*Little Ellie Claus*
Christopher Radko Ornament Offer
P.O. Box **7777-J90**
Mt. Prospect, IL  60056